PUSHOVER

ALSO BY LILLIAN O'DONNELL

A Private Crime
A Wreath for the Bride
A Good Night to Kill
The Other Side of the Door
Casual Affairs
Ladykiller
Cop Without a Shield
The Children's Zoo
Wicked Designs
Falling Star
No Business Being a Cop
Aftershock
Leisure Dying
The Baby Merchants
Dial 577-R-A-P-E
Don't Wear Your Wedding Ring
The Phone Calls
Dive into Darkness
The Face of the Crime
The Tachi Tree
The Sleeping Beauty Murders
The Babes in the Woods
Death of a Player
Murder Under the Sun
Death Schuss
Death Blanks the Screen
Death on the Grass

PUSHOVER

by

Lillian O'Donnell

G. P. PUTNAM'S SONS

New York

G. P. Putnam's Sons
Publishers Since 1838
200 Madison Avenue
New York, NY 10016

Library of Congress Cataloging-in-Publication Data

O'Donnell, Lillian.
Pushover / Lillian O'Donnell.
p.   cm.
ISBN 0-399-13674-6 (alk. paper)
I. Title.
PS3565.D59P8   1992   91-30205 CIP
813'.54—dc20

Printed in the United States of America
2   3   4   5   6   7   8   9   10

This book is printed on acid-free paper.
∞

PUSHOVER

—by—

Lillian O'Donnell

G. P. PUTNAM'S SONS

New York

G. P. Putnam's Sons
Publishers Since 1838
200 Madison Avenue
New York, NY 10016

Library of Congress Cataloging-in-Publication Data

O'Donnell, Lillian.
Pushover / Lillian O'Donnell.
p.   cm.
ISBN 0-399-13674-6 (alk. paper)
I. Title.
PS3565.D59P8   1992   91-30205 CIP
813'.54—dc20

Printed in the United States of America
2   3   4   5   6   7   8   9   10

This book is printed on acid-free paper.
∞

PUSHOVER

PROLOGUE

Though it was mid-October it felt like August. Dire predictions of a tropical-type disturbance—heavy downpours accompanied by dangerous lightning and thunder—induced many of the big companies in Manhattan to send their employees home early. Nevertheless, at five-forty-five P.M. the subway platforms were still crowded. It was almost impossible to move; to get on a train or off it. Despite the preoccupation with the weather and the acute discomfort, the crowd was wary, ready to fend off anybody who got too free with his hands.

On the lower level of the Fifty-ninth Street and Lexington Avenue station, a young black man strummed a medley of Caribbean tunes on a guitar. A few passengers dropped coins into the musician's upturned cap that lay on the floor at his feet, but most passed him by not listening to his music but trying to identify by direction of sound which train was coming in—uptown or down. A few stepped to the edge of the platform to take a look into the tunnel to see if, indeed, there was a train on the way, but they stepped back again quickly.

"Watch who you're shoving!"

Thelma Harrison cringed.

He snarled at her, malevolent eyes flashing out of a dirty face, tattered rags fluttering in the rush of air created by the oncoming train.

He hadn't washed in days, Thelma thought, but under the encrusted layers he was certainly white. As for age, he could be anything between twenty-five and fifty; the lines and furrows could be due to inner rage; his hair was hidden under a knitted cap pulled well down over his forehead. He held himself in a half crouch so that his height was also uncertain, and beneath the scarecrow rags he might have been fat or thin. Leather sandals revealed bare feet that were long and bony, suggesting a tall and lanky frame. In the old days he would have been called a vagrant or a derelict. Today, he was one of the homeless.

Thelma Harrison was twenty-two, the energetic, ambitious daughter of a small-town dentist. Medium height, plump but not fat, she had dark brown hair that was a mass of tight, frizzed curls. Her eyes were brown, large, always alert, intensely alive. Vivacity was part of her attraction. She had been a nurse on the staff of her hometown hospital. She was well liked and in all probability would have become head nurse, but she wanted more. To get it, she had to leave. Her parents, Monica and Donald Harrison, didn't try to dissuade her.

Thelma had been in New York just under two years. She was making good money as a special nurse, had a nice apartment, joined a health club, and the Metropolitan Museum. Like many single women in the big city, Thelma was looking for a "relationship." So far, she hadn't found the right man.

"I'm very sorry," she said to the homeless man whose eyes held her transfixed. "I didn't mean to bump into you. I didn't realize I'd done it."

"You done it all right. You pushed me."

Thelma was meeting a friend for dinner and so she had changed out of her uniform. She was wearing a new dress, a dark green coat style with a double row of gold buttons. Several gold chains were looped around her neck. The outfit suited her and she knew it and carried herself with pride. She had been warned by her friends that those chains around her neck were trouble. She had gone on wearing them—to show she had control of her own destiny, or as a challenge? She wasn't sure which, but at this moment, confronted by the shambling creature, she regretted it. His rage, she thought, was out of all proportion to the offense, fancied or otherwise. But he couldn't be after the chains; if he'd wanted them, he would long since have yanked them from her and run.

"I'm really very sorry. I didn't mean to. Excuse me."

She faltered because she realized suddenly, even as she apologized, that this was no random incident with a mentally disturbed person. The man had deliberately created an excuse for the confrontation. She turned away, intending to get as far from him as fast as she could, but with the roar of an oncoming train the crowd surged forward toward the edge of the platform to make sure of getting on as soon as the doors opened and they carried her back to him.

He grinned as once more they stood face-to-face. In that moment, despite the caked dirt, wild hair, and manic gleam in his eyes, Thelma knew him.

She spoke but couldn't hear her own voice over the roar of the train as it entered the station.

He said something and stretched out a hand.

She backed away. Her rear foot reached into a void and she screamed as she fell into the path of the oncoming train.

Few people heard the scream and only those who had been standing beside Thelma Harrison knew she had gone over the edge. The engineer brought the train to a stop only halfway into the station, but it was too late. The train doors were kept closed; the power was turned off. Metal gates were drawn across the exits at either end of the platform. By the time the Transit Authority police arrived, the confusion among the passengers on the train and those on the platform bordered on panic.

While they waited for the ES and EMS units, the Transit Police questioned witnesses and took names and addresses. Nobody had seen anything. A nearby homeless man didn't seem to understand the questions put to him. He cringed under the insistent repetition as though he was afraid he would be physically abused. The cops gave up and moved on to somebody at least coherent.

Obviously, the passengers on the train hadn't seen anything, and so the doors were opened at last. They literally surged out, fighting their way to the stairs and up to the street. Their principal concern was to find an alternate way home.

NURSE FALLS TO TRACKS IN PATH OF SUBWAY TRAIN

Straphanger nightmare

Thousands of commuters were trapped in sweltering, pitch-black subway cars when a woman fell or was pushed to the tracks in front of an oncoming train. Power was shut down on the IRT lines 4, 5, 6 for more than an hour, stopping trains in both directions between Fifty-ninth and Eighty-sixth Streets, as well as the N and R lines into Queens. About four thousand passengers were affected.

The victim was rushed to St. Luke's-Roosevelt Hospital where she was pronounced Dead on Arrival.

The story was limited to a brief paragraph on an inside page of the local tabloid. It didn't rate mention on radio or television. People pitching off platforms was no longer big news.

The TA conducted a routine investigation. Despite the number of people present, no one had noticed either the victim or the perpetrator, if there was a perpetrator. No one could say whether the unfortunate woman had fallen or been pushed. Interviews with her friends, which were conducted later, indicated that Thelma Harrison was well balanced, content in her work, and had no reason to commit suicide. There was nothing to go on. Nothing.

Chapter ONE

The mild weather continued into November. Winter loomed, but the temperature hovered in the sixties and bubbled over into the seventies. Some complained it was unhealthy; nevertheless, everyone enjoyed it.

The regular Sunday-night bridge game broke up early. The rubbers had been short, not very interesting, and the foursome didn't linger over the customary coffee, pastry, and conversation. Their hostess, the queen of their social group, made it clear she wanted them to go. She intended to get up early on Monday and she needed her rest. No longer did Wilma Danay, star of the silver screen, stay up till the small hours talking about the old days, sipping brandy in front of the television set, or dozing over a crossword puzzle. She no longer slept till noon. Now she had a reason to get up. It mattered whether the sun shone in the morning. Once again life had focus.

Grimacing with the effort, beads of sweat on his brow, Peter Bouchard hoisted himself out of the chair, which among the fragile French antiques had been specially reenforced for his two hundred and seventy pounds. Only those who had known him in the years of his youth and fame and the dedicated film buffs of the silents and the early talkies could discern the outlines of the once devastatingly handsome leading man.

"You could bring the boy with you," Bouchard urged as they lingered at the front door. "Why not?"

"Because he'd be bored out of his skull, that's why not," Wilma Danay retorted. "For God's sake, Peter, what would a ten-year-old boy do at a poetry reading? No, tomorrow's a school holiday, so we're going to the zoo in the morning and then I'm taking him to see the Teenage Mutant Ninja Turtles."

"You're going to do what? I wouldn't have believed it!" the actor intoned in his famous low timbered voice.

"Nor would I," the star, the living legend, agreed. Pleasure suffused the classic dignity with which she habitually carried herself and brought light to her heavy-lidded, sultry eyes.

Camilla Bouchard, looking almost ethereal next to her husband's bulk, embraced her and kissed her cheek. "Come on, Peter, let Wilma get to bed."

"So, next week it's my place." Nick Kouriades, costume and set designer for some of Wilma Danay's biggest hits, took his turn at the goodbye kiss.

"No, come here," Wilma said. "I don't want to leave the boy alone."

Kouriades's thick black eyebrows went up. "I thought he was only staying over the weekend."

"Well, this time he's staying longer. Adele would like to be able to leave him with me and then pick him up, shuttle him back and forth at her convenience. But that's not the way it's going to be. A child should have a stable home environment. If she can't provide it, I will."

They'd heard it all before. They disapproved, but nobody said anything. Wilma Danay was eighty-four with neither the strength nor the temperament to take on a ten-year-old boy. These three relics of their own past—Kouriades, seventy-five; Camilla Bouchard, fifty-five; Peter Bouchard, eighty-two—were accustomed to deferring to her in all things. To them she was still the star and they the supporting players. Only Bouchard, the last of her leading men still alive, had the courage to challenge her, sometimes. He started to speak, but at a look from his wife remained silent.

Having seen them out, Wilma Danay carefully locked the door. Thirty years ago when the building went up, she had bought the seven-room apartment for one hundred and fifty thousand dollars, a lot of money in those days. Now it was worth a couple of million, not counting the added value her name would attach to it. There had never been a security problem in the building. Daily, she read horror stories about break-ins, robberies, muggings in lobbies and elevators, but no such thing happened here. Doormen were on duty around the clock. They knew the tenants and the regular visitors, and no stranger got past them. During the day, Wilma Danay and her companion used the lower lock only. At night, she made sure the dead lock was engaged as well. She never bothered with the chain.

After securing the door, she paused to look at herself in the antique mirror in the hall. Pink-shaded wall sconces gave off a glow calculated to soften the age lines even the best facials and most expensive creams could not erase. Though she knew she wasn't facing reality, Wilma Danay was pleased by what she saw. She turned off the rest of the lights in the front one by one till everything in both the hall and the vast salon was out and then, again part of the ritual, she stood for a moment to look out at the sweeping view of the Manhattan skyline, contemplating the brilliance and power of the city she, an uneducated girl from Minnesota, had conquered. Tonight the moon was full and high in a clear sky, its silver light reflecting on the river, filling the room. She thought back to the years of her success with satisfaction and without regret for having retired early. There had been a time when she'd had doubts. None of her marriages had been successful. Her maternal instincts weren't strong, and when her only daughter left home first for college and then to get married, Wilma Danay gave up even the pretense of a family life. When Todd was born, everything changed.

Turning down the inner hall to her bedroom, Wilma Danay stopped at the boy's door. No light showed underneath, but she knocked anyway.

"Todd?"

No answer.

She turned the knob and entered quietly.

There was a dark lump in the middle of the bed and a faint glow of light showed at the edges of the covers. She smiled to herself. "Todd?"

The flashlight went out instantly. The lump flattened.

"What did I tell you about reading in bed?" She put on the lamp on the night stand.

The boy rolled over, blinking. "Tomorrow's a holiday, Nana, Veterans Day. I can sleep late," Todd Millard reminded his grandmother.

"What've you got under the pillow?"

The boy looked down sheepishly. He was a stocky child with a broad, triangular face, high forehead and pointed chin, hazel eyes set widely apart, and thick blond hair. He was a thoughtful child, and his grandmother loved to watch him as he reasoned through a problem. Wilma Danay had married three times, each marriage ending in the divorce court. Each husband had unlocked a different side of Wilma's nature: Quentin Noble, when she met him a far bigger star than she, showed her passion; Peter Bouchard, although never professionally her equal, taught her style and the value of the intellect; but her first husband, Frank Grillo, had given her what counted the most—a daughter, Adele, and through her this grandson.

"Come on, Todd, hand it over."

"Oh, Nana, gee . . . I'm at the best part." Making a face, he reached under the pillow and pulled out the forbidden comic book.

She made a face back at him. "Tomorrow we'll go to the bookstore and select something more suitable for you."

He groaned. "Not like *Heidi.*"

"No, that's a girl's book. I made a mistake, okay? It'll be something you'll enjoy; I promise. Something by Jules Verne maybe. Science fiction?" She responded quickly to his scowl. "And from now on when there's no school the next day, we'll extend the lights out to ten. How's that? Deal?"

"Deal."

She tucked him in, bent over, and kissed him. "Sleep tight."

As she reached the door, he called out. "Nana? Superman has just been captured. Could I take a quick peek to see how he gets away?"

"Tomorrow," she said, and switched off the light and pulled the door gently shut.

In her own room, Wilma Danay took off the blue velvet hostess gown with gold braid trim and put on a creamy satin and lace nightgown. Though she'd been sleeping alone for more years than she was willing to admit, Wilma Danay still prepared herself for bed with the meticulous care she would have if expecting a lover. Seated at her vanity, she removed all her makeup; the older one got, the better one looked without it, she mused. Her beauty, now as in her youth, consisted chiefly in the sharp delineation of features—high cheek bones, chiseled nose, sculpted lips, and the fine, translucent, unblemished skin of which she had taken almost obsessive care, shielding it from the sun long before the skin cancer scare. Her hair, once chestnut, was now almost completely gray, but to color it would have been a useless vanity. At eighty-four, whom did you fool? As she brushed the long, still-shining tresses, she thought she heard a buzz at her front door. It had been very soft, so she stopped brushing in order to listen. She'd just about decided she'd made a mistake or else someone was ringing the next apartment, when she heard it again. Reaching for the satin robe that matched her nightgown, she went out through the corridor and the living room to the foyer. She stood well back from the door and called out.

"Who is it?"

"Delivery."

"I didn't order anything. You have the wrong apartment."

"Danay? 1414?"

"Yes, but there's a mistake. I didn't order anything."

"Anchovy pizza from Pizza Palace."

"Oh." She'd ordered from them on occasion, for Todd mainly. Todd loved anchovy pizza. Could he have called out while they were playing bridge and forgotten to mention it? Not likely. It was a mixup, that was all, but it made her nervous. Also, how had the delivery man gotten upstairs without being announced? That frightened her.

"You have the wrong apartment," she called out firmly. "You'll have to go back down and check with the doorman." Quickly, tiptoeing as though the man outside could hear and know what she was doing, Wilma Danay went into the kitchen, picked up the house phone, and dialed the night doorman. He didn't answer. One ring, two, three . . . *Oh, God, where are you, Bert?* If Bert was on his meal break, then his relief should be picking up. While the phone continued to ring, she heard the click of a key in the lock. From where she stood she could see the front door, and the moonlight glinted off the brass knob as it turned.

Quietly, she put the receiver back in its cradle. Then she slid out the cutlery drawer and fumbled inside. She wanted the carving knife, but all that came to hand was a serrated steak knife. Good enough, she thought. Clenching it behind her, she watched in horrid fascination as the front door opened and a man entered. He stood just inside. He held a pizza box in both hands and looked around uncertainly. He was big and he wore a stocking mask.

"Who are you?" Wilma Danay trembled. Her voice was so hoarse she could hardly speak. "What do you want?"

He kicked the door shut behind him.

"What do you want?" she repeated, desperation giving her courage. "Take whatever you want. I won't stop you. I won't call the police even after you're gone. I promise."

He wasn't listening; he was still looking around. "What's down there?" He pointed behind her.

"The pantry and the kitchen." Wilma Danay answered automatically. It was almost as though he were getting his bearings, she thought. "Look, if you'll just tell me . . ."

"Where's the boy?"

He was bigger than she'd realized. He loomed over her. The stocking mask flattened his features and distorted his voice. He was like a Frankenstein and at the same time he looked ludicrous holding that pizza box. She had a nervous urge to giggle.

"Where's his room?"

She gasped instead. An icy chill went through her. Now, she understood. "What boy?" The actress fell back on her skills. "There's no boy here. Only me. I'm alone. Please, take what you want." She pointed to the console at the end of the foyer. "There's five hundred dollars in cash in the drawer. Take it." He didn't move. "I have jewelry . . . in the study . . . this way." No longer concerned for herself, she was trying to lead the man away from Todd.

"Where's the boy?"

"I have some very valuable things." Wilma Danay was negotiating. "Come on, I'll show you." Her plan was to lead him to the study. She would open the safe for him. She hoped that while he was preoccupied looking through it, she could quietly slip away, get out of the apartment and into the hall where her screams would be heard. "This way," she urged.

Neither one of them thought of turning on the lights; Wilma Danay was well accustomed to the placement of her furniture and there was enough moonlight for the intruder to follow her.

"Come on."

Maybe she was too eager. Somehow, she must have given it away because suddenly the man stopped and looked down the other corridor.

"What's over there?"

"Nothing. My bedroom. I don't keep valuables there."

"And that other room?"

She shrugged. "A spare room."

"Let's take a look."

She ran ahead and stood in front of Todd's door. "No."

"Step aside."

She didn't move. As he reached to push her out of the way, Wilma Danay brought out the knife she'd been hiding behind her, raised it high, and made a wild lunge. The blade caught him in the left shoulder, glancing off the collar bone.

"Agh . . ." He groaned in pain and anger and dropped the pizza to clutch at the wound. "Witch," he snarled as he examined the blood on his fingers. "You old witch."

Terrified at what she'd done, Wilma Danay cowered but stood her ground.

"I told you to get out of my way." Using his right hand, he administered a vicious blow to the jaw that sent the aged actress reeling. But before he could open the door of Todd's room, she collected herself and flung herself at his feet, wrapping her arms around his legs.

"Lock the door, Todd," she screamed. "Lock the door! Don't come out!"

"Shut up," the intruder hissed. Despite the intensity of his rage he remembered to keep his voice down.

"Help! Help!" Wilma Danay screamed as loud as she could. No one would hear; the walls were concrete, just about soundproof. She knew that, but he didn't and he was getting very nervous. His body was drenched. Beads of sweat oozed through the stocking mask.

It was the sweat of anger and fear rather than effort. Wilma Danay could smell the fear and it encouraged her to continue to resist. She tightened her hold on his legs, hung on them like dead weight. He tried to pry her loose. As he unwrapped one arm, she tightened her hold with the other. He tried to kick free; the points of his cowboy boots caught her in the abdomen. Pain caused the blackness around her to splinter into shards of green and violet and orange light. Somehow, using him for support, grabbing at his clothes, she managed to pull herself to her feet.

"Help!" she screamed one last time, and making claws out of her long, beautifully manicured nails, she raked them right through the stocking mask into his skin from his brow, over his eyes, gouging his cheeks till the blood spurted.

Half blinded, snarling with pain, he grabbed her and literally threw her down the hall. With the last vestige of her strength, Wilma Danay picked herself up and ran into her bedroom to the window. She tried to raise it so she could call out, but it wouldn't budge. While she struggled with it, he was on her. Her last, futile scream was smothered as he caught her from behind and covered her mouth. She thrashed and flailed for a short time and then stopped. Just gave up and went limp.

"You're going to pay for this, bitch. Oh yes, you'll pay, and the price just went up."

She didn't respond. She offered no more resistance. He shook her. Nothing. Cautiously, he took his hand from her mouth. Silence. She's passed out, he thought, and contemptuously tossed her to one side.

"Okay, kid, open up." He kicked at the door of the boy's room. "We don't have time for games, kid. Daddy's waiting." Getting no response to that either, the intruder moved back a few steps and charged. The lock gave way and the door flew open.

Inside it was totally dark; not only was the light out but the shades had been drawn so that no moonlight entered.

The intruder blinked a couple of times. The actress's finger nails had dug deep and the blood stung his eyes. Some of it had clotted on the nylon of the mask so that it was like a blindfold. He grasped the bottom of the stocking and pulled it off over his head. He still couldn't see. "Where are the lights, for God's sake?"

While he floundered, feeling along the wall for the switch, Todd Millard darted from the far side of the bed where he'd been crouching and darted out the open door.

"Nana?"

Her bedroom was dark, but a shaft of moonlight revealed his grandmother lying on the floor motionless.

Behind him, the lights of his own room went on.

Instinctively, he turned, and for a long moment he stared into the intruder's gouged and blood-streaked face. The child and the killer were locked in each other's gaze. Then Todd ran. He ran as fast as his ten-year-old legs could carry him.

Chapter
TWO

As Norah Mulcahaney walked up the steps and entered the
Seventh Regiment Armory on Park Avenue she instantly felt
the excitement. Sally Felix certainly knew how to throw a
party, she thought and took the elevator to the fourth-floor
mess. Laughter and music greeted her when she got off.
Already, the lounge area was crowded. Uniforms abounded.
Obviously, most of the guests had come directly from the
ceremonies, as Norah had herself. Today marked the first
graduation of police officers since the new police commissioner took office. It had been held in the main gym of St.
John's University. The class consisted of seven hundred and
thirteen, comprising four hundred and seventy-five men and
two hundred and thirty-eight women. Most of the rookies
would be assigned to the new Community Patrol Officer
Program. Some of them were pleased; others were not.

"Patrol is going to become the heart and soul of the new
NYPD," the mayor had proclaimed in his speech to the
graduates.

Some believed that; others remained skeptical.

The site for the party had been shrewdly selected. It was
large enough so that there was no risk of leaving anyone out.
It was historic, the home of the famed Rainbow Division.

The young queen of England and her consort had reviewed troops in the drill shed at the back of the building. It offered a sense of tradition that appealed to the brass and also to the young graduates. A five-piece combo playing with enthusiasm dispelled any initial awkwardness between them. Sally Felix, wife of Bureau Chief James Felix, was throwing the party to honor her niece, Kathryn Webber, a member of the graduating class.

Norah Mulcahaney had not expected such a crowd; there must be nearly two hundred people here, she estimated, a judicious mix of police and civilians. As wife of a three-star chief, Sally could have reached all the way up to the PC himself, who would certainly have put in at least a brief appearance. But Sally had resisted the temptation. She knew that the presence of top brass would dampen the spirits of the new recruits, make them nervous and ill at ease. Also, it wouldn't do her niece any good. Norah wasn't so naive as to believe that the party was intended solely as celebration. Instructors from the Academy were present, as well as classmates of Officer Webber, and the rank and file from the Twentieth Precinct to which she had been assigned. The highest ranking officer was Chief Felix himself. He was a relative, so it wasn't showing off. As Norah watched, Sally Felix supervised the enlarging of the dancing area. Her red hair was threaded with gray and cut in a short, shining cap. Her dark eyes sparkled. She had, Norah thought, steered a course between beer and champagne tastes.

"Get you a drink, Lieutenant?"

Norah turned around. "Roy! Good to see you. How are you? Not that I need to ask. You look great."

Roy Brennan was an old friend. He and Norah Mulcahaney had worked together first out of Homicide North. Then when that prestigious command, along with Homicide South, had been divided, they had both been assigned to the

Fourth Zone. They both still worked out of the same precinct, but Roy, now also a lieutenant, was back in uniform and downstairs and Norah was upstairs commanding the Fourth. They rarely saw each other anymore.

"How's Grace?" Norah looked around. "I don't see her."

"She's home. We couldn't get a baby-sitter."

"I'm sorry."

Roy grinned. "She's expecting."

"Again?" Norah's face lit up. Brennan, a dour man who had seemed destined for permanent bachelorhood, had at forty-two suddenly fallen in love. He'd married and immediately started a family. He had two boys. "Congratulations. You sure are making up for lost time."

Brennan blushed. It made his freckles stand out. He didn't look like he was nudging fifty. "How is it with you, Norah?"

"Good. Good."

Six months ago Randall Tye, a well-known television newsman and anchor, had been killed. Brennan knew that Norah had cared deeply for him; had, in fact, been on the verge of marrying him. He and Grace had attended Tye's funeral. They had offered condolences then; there was no need to say any more, to reopen the wound, but he did look at her searchingly.

Norah Mulcahaney was in uniform today as he was himself. She wore it well, Roy thought, wore it with pride, holding herself straight and erect to her full five foot eight. From a shy rookie, she had developed into an expert investigator and strong administrator. In the two and a half years she'd been running the Fourth Division Homicide Squad, Norah had had to face ugly scenes and make tough decisions, but she'd never lost her compassion. That was her distinguishing characteristic. Roy remembered when she was younger how her square jaw would suddenly jut out in defiance and her blue eyes flash with determination, sometimes called stubbornness by her superiors. The jaw seemed less prominent, he thought, and her blue eyes perhaps a little less intense—call them more tranquil. Not resigned though. Never resigned.

Norah's husband, Captain Joseph Antony Capretto, had also died violently. At the time, Norah's reaction had been to get away, to turn her back on the horror of Joe's death and of all the others she faced on The Job. She'd taken a temporary leave, but that wasn't the answer. She discovered she had nothing to take the place of The Job. It was the mainstay of her life.

Four years, arrid and lonely, passed before she met Randall Tye and now he was gone, too. She hadn't even thought of turning her back on what had happened; she'd had no intention of running away. On the contrary, though it appeared that Randall had died of a self-administered drug overdose, Norah refused to believe it. She was convinced the cocaine had been administered against his will with the intent to kill. In spite of opposition that reached as high as the C of D (Chief of Detectives), Norah had refused to step aside and let someone else handle the investigation. Not this time.

She'd dedicated herself to finding Randall's killer. In the course of her inquiry she had discovered a money-laundering operation that involved political and government figures. She received a commendation and had been advised that if she took the captain's exam and did as well as expected, she would be given a quick appointment. So far, Roy Brennan had not heard that Norah was doing anything about it.

There were lines around her eyes, Brennan noted, and gray in her shining dark hair that was sometimes almost black and other times closer to chestnut, depending on the light. She usually wore it severely pulled back and tied with a colorful scarf, but today because she was in uniform she used a plain barrette. Norah's getting on, Roy thought. Like the rest of us! She must be looking at forty. It was hard to think of Norah Mulcahaney as anything but an eager recruit. She was, in fact, a seasoned veteran.

"How about that drink?" Brennan asked. "White wine?"

At her nod he made his way to the bar and within a couple of minutes was back with a glass for her. "Why don't you come over for dinner some night? Grace would love to see you."

"This is hardly the time for Grace to be struggling with a dinner party."

"Are you kidding? I never in my life saw a woman with whom pregnancy agrees more. No morning sickness. She's literally blooming. And her energy . . . !" He threw up the free hand.

"Nice party."

Captain Emanuel Jacoby, commanding officer of the Two-Oh, joined them. He was short, paunchy, balding, not an impressive figure, but his people knew him to be capable, strict—even demanding, but fair. He would not tolerate laziness, was impatient with ineptitude, but if you did your job you wouldn't have any problem with the captain.

"Have you met Officer Webber?" Jacoby asked Norah.

"Yes. As a matter of fact, twice before. Once when she was preparing her application, then after she was accepted. Sally Felix asked me to talk to her, to tell her what police work is all about. Deglamorize it. I did my best, but it didn't have the effect Sally was after."

Norah and the two men looked across the room to where the new officer stood surrounded. She noticed they were looking and disengaged herself.

"She's coming over," Brennan said.

Kathryn Webber was medium height, slim, graceful. She had a pale, narrow face. Her hair was a silver blonde, fine and naturally curly. Her green eyes were shining, darting from one group to another as she made her way to them.

Norah was not misled by her soft appearance. She knew something about the rookie cop's background and a lot about the will that had brought her this far. Kathryn was twenty-two; she came from Boston. She had an older brother, Brian, who was a member of the Boston Police force. As a little girl, Kathryn had idolized Brian, followed at his heels like a puppy, wanted to do everything he did. Like most older brothers, Brian was embarrassed to have his little sister tagging along. When Kathryn announced she intended to join the Boston Police, too, he was appalled. He tried to discourage her; the family tried. But Kathryn was used to getting her way. She struck a deal. She would finish college; that satisfied her parents, somewhat. She would not apply to the Boston Police. That pacified Brian. However, she would go to New York, take up residence, and apply to the New York Police Academy. Aunt Sally Felix lived in New York. Her husband, Chief James Felix, was top brass in the NYPD. They would surely be willing to keep an eye on her, she pointed out.

What could the family or Brian say?

Norah couldn't help but be impressed by her determination.

The rookie, standing straight and proud in her uniform, smiled and held out her hand.

"Hello, Lieutenant Mulcahaney. It's nice to see you again. Thank you for coming."

"My pleasure, Kathryn. Captain Jacoby, Lieutenant Brennan, this is Officer Kathryn Webber."

"Congratulations." They nodded and smiled.

There was an awkward pause. Brennan looked at his glass, which he had barely touched. "Ladies, can I get you anything? Captain?"

Norah shook her head as did Kathryn Webber. Manny Jacoby, not at his best in large gatherings, was already backing toward escape. "I have to leave, I'm afraid. Again, congratulations, Officer Webber. Wonderful party."

He shook hands with her. Brennan in the guise of accompanying Jacoby, also got away. The two women were left standing alone.

"I didn't want Aunt Sally to do anything this elaborate," the new officer confided. "All these people. I know if it weren't for Uncle Jim they wouldn't be here. I'm embarrassed. But I'm glad you could make it, Norah."

"I wouldn't have missed it. And don't be embarrassed. There are other parties like this and the brass that's here will drop in on them later."

"I see." It didn't appear to make her feel better, though. "Anyway, I did want to tell you how happy I am to be assigned to the Two-Oh with you. Of course, I know I won't be working with you. I didn't mean that," she gushed. "We probably won't even see each other except in the hall or the ladies' room, but just knowing you're there, upstairs, will be reassuring."

"Good." What else was there to say, Norah thought.

"May I ask a favor, Norah? If I get into difficulty, if I should need advice, may I . . . ."

Norah didn't like the way this was going. "If you need advice or have any kind of problem, you should go to your sergeant," she said, while at the same time trying not to appear to be repulsing the girl.

"That's procedure, I know that. What I mean is . . . if I should need a woman's advice."

Jaw tight, blue eyes narrowed, Norah looked hard at the rookie. "I don't think you need to worry about anything like that."

"No, I didn't mean . . ."

"Don't go looking for trouble, Kathryn."

"I wasn't alluding to sexual discrimination."

A waitress approached. "Lieutenant Mulcahaney? Phone call for you. I'll show you."

"Thank you. Excuse me, Kathryn." Norah followed the waitress. She was glad to get away.

The complaint was called in to 911 at ten-forty-five P.M. The caller reported a crime in progress and requested immediate assistance. RMP (Radio Motor Patrol) reached the scene at ten-fifty-seven. It was too late. They advised Communications. Communications in turn made the necessary notifications, starting with a call to the Fourth Division, and Detective First Grade Simon Wyler caught the squeal.

A sudden and violent death was routinely investigated, usually by the detective initially on the scene. However, as soon as Wyler learned the name of the victim, he knew this would be a big case, so before leaving the squad he called Lieutenant Mulcahaney's home. She didn't answer. That meant she was still at the party, having a good time. She deserved it. He'd get on over to the scene and check it out. By the time he did that and somebody from the ME's office showed up for the preliminary medical, the lieut' could have a couple of extra hours to forget her troubles.

Simon Wyler had had a variety of assignments before coming to the Fourth: Safe and Loft, Community Relations, Narcotics, but he hadn't been totally satisfied with any. It didn't take more than a week into his first case at the Fourth to know he had found his spot. Norah Mulcahaney, herself newly head of the squad, sensed it, too. Wyler was tall, flashy on the exterior, a jaunty dresser with a variety of interests and a girlfriend to match each. But underneath, Simon Wyler was a thorough, patient, serious investigator, and Norah gave him leeway. He was aware of it and was grateful.

Detective Wyler arrived at the elegant building on Sixty-fourth Street just fifteen minutes after getting the notification. He admired the pebbled Japanese garden with lighted fountain at the center, the circular drive, and the columned portico. He was impressed by the marble lobby and the uniformed doorman wearing spotless white gloves. The inside man, also wearing gloves, was holding one of a bank of three elevators for him.

"Fourteenth floor, Officer."

The lights were blazing when Simon Wyler entered Wilma Danay's apartment. A couple of overturned chairs, a pair of shattered china figurines, were the initial indications a struggle had taken place. Next, he spotted a knife lying a short way down a hall off to the left of the living room. He went over and bent down to look at it more closely. The tip was bloody, suggesting it had not penetrated deeply. What piqued Wyler's interest was a squashed carton of pizza a few feet past the knife. It had been stepped on and a trail of yellow and red led to a bedroom farther down the hall. The door was open. Wyler went in.

The legendary star of the silver screen was a scrawny old woman in a torn satin nightgown and robe. Battered, bruised, her shriveled breasts exposed, her long gray hair loose around her, she lay on the floor at the foot of a king-sized bed, a travesty of youth.

She had been brutally mauled, but as far as he could see no skin was broken, so the blood on the knife must be the intruder's. She was the one who had inflicted the wound. She had put up a real fight. Good for her, Simon thought, and headed for a phone.

Norah got her coat and then looked around for Jim or Sally Felix. She couldn't see either. If she left without saying goodbye and thanking them, they'd understand of course, but . . . Then she caught sight of Kathryn on the crowded dance floor. Her head was thrown back; her eyes were alight. At last, she was enjoying herself. She was having fun without worrying about the impression she was making. Norah was glad for her.

She cut her way through to her. "Kathryn, would you tell Sally and the inspector that I had to leave?" She didn't say why; it would be understood.

For a moment Norah thought she detected a glint of envy in the rookie's green eyes. Then Kathryn's partner reached for her and they resumed their dance. Imagination, Norah decided. What she'd seen was a reflection of her own feelings, her nostalgia for the days when she was young and at the threshold of her life and her career.

Chapter

THREE

Even in death we are not equal. Even in death there are priorities. Because the direct cause was not readily apparent, but mainly because the victim was an international celebrity, a woman whose life had been first conducted in a blaze of notoriety and then shrouded in mystery, Phillip Worgan, chief medical examiner of the City of New York, responded personally to the call. He was at the scene well before Norah Mulcahaney. He finished quickly, but told that she was on her way, he waited.

Having been briefed by Wyler over the telephone, Norah quickly confirmed what he'd told her, and then catching sight of Worgan, she joined him and together they looked down at the sprawled figure of the woman who had been known and envied by millions.

"Did you ever see any of her pictures?" Worgan asked.

"Virgin Queen, Comrade Anna," Norah recalled.

The ME nodded. *"Comrade Anna* was my favorite. I've seen it at least a half dozen times on the late movie and I've got it on tape. She played it so straight and yet managed an undercurrent of humor." He shook his head, marveling. "She was a superb actress and one of the most beautiful of women. Look at the bone structure—high brow, perfect nose and cheek bones. And look at the skin; even at her age—translucent."

"I didn't know you were a movie buff, Phil."

"I was a fan of Wilma Danay's. She used to walk in the park around the reservoir every morning, rain or shine. If I was in the area I used to take a run myself just to get a look at her. But we never spoke. I can't tell you how many times I was tempted."

"Not wise to walk alone in the park," Norah commented.

"I'm going back a few years," he replied. "I don't think she did much walking anywhere lately. She was getting frail. You can see for yourself."

Both looked down once more, their silence a tribute. Worgan sighed heavily.

"I can't tell you how she died. I *can* tell you how she didn't. She wasn't knifed, or strangled. On closer examination we may find a bullet wound, but I doubt it." He paused.

"She took a brutal battering, but she put up a valiant resistance. There are scrapings under her nails of the assailant's skin as well as nylon threads that indicate he was wearing a stocking mask. Strands of his hair are clenched in her hands. There's plenty of blood—some of it possibly hers, most of it surely his." Worgan sighed again. "Sad for such a woman to go like this."

"She was in her nightgown so the perp' didn't follow her on the street and push his way in after her," Norah observed. "With the kind of security in this building that's not likely, anyway."

"You think she admitted him?" Worgan looked down at the cardboard box and the mashed pizza. "To deliver that?"

"Maybe. At this point we're guessing."

Worgan grinned sheepishly. Usually it was Norah who tried to get information out of him. "So we'll be in touch."

"As soon as either of us has anything."

At Worgan's signal the orderlies prepared the body, placed it on the gurney, and strapped it in. He followed them out.

Norah waited till the front door was closed before joining Simon Wyler. "What've you got?"

"According to the 911 operator, a kid put in the complaint."

"Kid?"

"A boy. Sounded young, the operator said." Wyler consulted his notebook. "The kid said: 'A man's hitting my grandma. She's screaming. Please come right away!' He gave this address and this apartment number."

"Where is he now?"

Wyler shrugged. "Nobody knows. There was nobody here when Pasternak arrived." He indicated one of the uniforms.

John Pasternak was big, blond, and good-looking. In the course of years on radio patrol he had answered all kinds of complaints, from domestic disputes and drug-related situations, to medical emergencies. He had entered tenements, public housing projects, and luxury high rises. He could read and interpret the crime scene as well as most detectives. He was well aware that the death of Wilma Danay had not yet been labeled a homicide, but he had no doubt that it would be.

"How long after the call did you arrive?" Norah asked.

Though he had the answer pat, the patrolman nevertheless consulted his notebook. "My partner and I entered the building at precisely ten-fifty-seven P.M. We informed the doorman of the complaint, but he didn't know anything about it. No one had called down to report a disturbance. We gave him the apartment number and he knew the tenant was Miss Danay. She'd had visitors earlier in the evening, but they'd left at approximately ten P.M. and no one had gone up since. We tried to reach her on the house phone, but no one answered, so we came up. The door was shut, locked automatically. We rang the doorbell. We knocked. We pounded. No response. There was no sound from inside. Breaking down the door would have been damage to private property." He appealed to Norah. "Whatever had happened was over. We didn't feel justified."

"So?"

"So my partner went down for the key. They didn't want to give it to him. Miss Danay was very big on privacy, and they didn't want us barging in and maybe embarrassing her. So we lost more time. Eighteen more minutes." He was clearly upset.

Norah didn't blame him. The Job was getting tougher all the time, she thought. Considered decisions were required in situations that in the past had triggered automatic responses. "Go on."

"Well, by the time we gained entry and found her . . ." He shook his head. "We put in a call for EMS and we tried CPR ourselves. It was no use."

"You did what you could," Norah offered. She would have liked to be able to offer more.

He knew it. "Thanks, Lieutenant."

She took a deep breath and indicated the sprung lock on the door opposite Wilma Danay's bedroom. "Did you do that?"

"No, ma'am. We found it like that."

"Where's the doorman?" she asked Wyler.

"Downstairs."

"Have him come up."

While Wyler was on the house phone in the pantry, Norah walked through the apartment; *took a tour* might better describe it, she thought as she wandered from one room to the next, seven in all, starting with the sumptuous salon. The

furniture there was sixteenth-century French—sofas, otto-
man, bergères upholstered in various shades of lavender,
surely authentic. They were arranged in conversation group-
ings around three large Aubussons. Then there were the
paintings. Norah was no expert but she could recognize a
Renoir and knew that it wasn't a copy any more than the
furniture was reproduction. She could also identify a Bonnard and a couple of Modiglianis, the knowledge a result of
museum dates with Randall Tye. The paintings covered the
walls of the main room and were everywhere throughout the
apartment.

To the right, a formal dining room could seat sixteen
under a glittering crystal chandelier. The kitchen was large
enough to serve twice that number, and the adjoining pantry
not to be found in modern residences. There was a den with
book stacks on one side and a television wall screen on the
other. Norah recrossed the salon to the bedroom wing, once
again entering the master suite where Wilma Danay met her
death. It included a dressing room and bath with sunken tub.
Opening the row of closets, Norah knew she was looking at
a lifetime's dedication to beautiful clothes. Wilma Danay
hadn't gotten rid of very much and Norah couldn't blame
her. The clothes that hung there were more like costumes
than everyday apparel. There was a timeless distinction
about them that identified them as the creation of talented
designers for one specific personality, for every possible occasion. There were furs, too, a fortune in furs—short, long,
coats, jackets, capes, each in its own ventilated storage bag.
Today such a collection would be denounced and the owner
labeled, at the least, as insensitive.

There should be a domestic, Norah thought; she couldn't
see Wilma Danay doing her own housework. The appointments of the next bedroom suggested a live-in housekeeper.
The furniture was solid, somber, probably from the star's

early, less affluent and less discriminating period. The clothes in that closet were classic, well-made and expensive. Hand-me-downs? The room was orderly with few personal touches. Instead of a dressing table there was a desk, clear except for a small, silver-framed photograph. It showed Wilma Danay and a woman about ten years younger posed in front of a Silver Ghost Rolls-Royce. The star wore an impeccably tailored pants suit, and though it was an informal snapshot, her stance was professional. The other woman, blonde hair piled high on top of her head, stood slightly apart as though ill at ease. If this woman—friend, relative, employee—lived in the apartment, then where had she been when Wilma Danay fought for her life? Where was she now?

Norah opened one of the desk drawers. It was crammed with makeup. She examined the jars and bottles, the lipsticks, eye shadows—cheap stuff, five-and-dime stuff.

Finally, having purposely left the room with the broken door for the last, Norah now felt ready to deal with it. The first thing she noted was blood on the knob.

"Check for fingerprints and get blood samples," she told Forensics, and went in.

It was an adult's room, but a youngster had been occupying it. School notebooks were on a long table in front of the window. A catcher's mitt lay on top of them. There was a television set, a VCR, and a shelf of cassettes. She looked in the closet and found a young boy's clothes: a warm-up suit, jeans, windbreaker. Skates, hockey sticks, baseball bats, and tennis rackets littered the floor. The bed had been slept in. There was a telephone on the night stand.

"Check this phone for prints," she told Forensics. Then she waved Officer Pasternak over. "Were the lights on when you entered?"

"At the front, no. I put them on. They weren't on in Miss Danay's room either. But they were on here."

"Okay." Again she spoke to Forensics. "Be sure to do this lightswitch."

"Lieutenant?" Simon Wyler looked in. "I have Mr. Kimmel, the night doorman."

"Good, good. I'll be there in a minute." But she stood considerably longer than that at the window looking out. Fourteen stories down, she thought, and no fire escape.

When she came out, she stopped for another look at the pizza trail on the plush ivory carpet. As she read it, the box had been dropped in the inner hall past the living room. There were no traces on the victim's feet, so it was the intruder who had stepped into it. The larger accumulations indicated where he had stopped and where the struggle had taken place; first, in the corridor and then at the foot of the bed in the master bedroom.

"Call the Pizza Palace," Norah directed Wyler. "Find out when the order was placed, by whom, and who delivered it."

"Right. Mr. Kimmel, Lieutenant?"

"I know. Yes."

So now she focused her attention on the doorman. Bert Kimmel was wiry, in his mid-sixties, probably close to seventy. His eyes were rheumy, lids puffed. An allergy or had he been crying?

He answered without being asked. "She was a lady, a real fine lady. I've worked here thirty years, since the building went up. Miss Danay was one of the first to move in. She knew every man on the staff—his name and circumstances. If anybody was sick or in any kind of trouble, she helped without being asked. And she didn't talk about it, either."

"She lived alone?"

"No, ma'am. There's a lady companion. Been with Miss Danay as far back as I know. Yolanda Yates. Used to be Miss Danay's secretary when she was still in pictures."

"How about domestics?"

"A cleaning woman comes in daily from nine to three except Sundays."

"I see a boy's things in one of the bedrooms—clothes, toys, sports equipment."

"Those would be Todd's. Todd Millard, Miss Danay's grandson. The parents are divorced. He stays over when his mother is away on a business trip."

"Does that happen often?"

"Sure does. He's here now."

"No, he isn't."

"I saw him with Miss Danay this afternoon. It was around five and they were coming in from the park. They looked like they'd had a real good time. They talked about what they would do tomorrow, it being a school holiday."

"And you haven't seen the boy since?"

"No, ma'am."

"What about Miss Yates, the lady companion? Was she supposed to be at home tonight?"

"No, ma'am. She went to visit her sister in Montreal."

"Did she visit her sister often?"

"Once a year when she took her vacation." Again, he answered promptly. "She got a message that her sister had been in an automobile accident."

Norah nodded; she didn't doubt his information. After a while the men who worked in these buildings achieved the status of friend and knew almost everything about the lives of the tenants. The more solitary the tenant, the more likely she was to confide and the more personal were the revelations likely to be.

"So Miss Danay was alone with the boy tonight?"

"No, ma'am, she had guests. Her regular Sunday-night bridge group. They took turns hosting the game. There was Mr. Bouchard—Peter Bouchard the actor—and Mrs. Bouchard, and Mr. Kouriades—the costume designer."

Kimmel announced the names with pride as though indeed these celebrities were personal friends.

"What time did the game break up?"

"Early. Usually they stayed till at least eleven. Tonight, it was close to ten. I'd just got back from my dinner break," he explained.

"And from then on Miss Danay had no other visitors?"

Kimmel shook his head.

Norah pointed to the pizza box on the floor. "Then how did that get here?"

Kimmel gawked. "I don't know."

"You're supposed to announce all visitors and all deliveries, aren't you?"

"Yes, ma'am." He turned a putty gray. "And I do. I'm real careful not to let strangers into the building. We've never had anything like this happen. You can ask anybody—the tenants, the management, the rest of the staff. Never. Never."

"I'm not accusing you of negligence, Mr. Kimmel. I'm trying to find out how the killer got in."

At that word the doorman began to tremble.

Norah pressed. "You never left your station?"

Kimmel flushed. "I stepped in the back to make a personal call. It only took a few minutes. I made sure to lock the lobby door first." He stopped, but he saw Norah wasn't satisfied. "My son has an alcohol problem. He was supposed to go to an AA meeting. I wanted to make sure he got home again safely."

"And had he?" Norah asked.

"Yes."

"That's good, Mr. Kimmel. That's a big step forward."

"Yes, ma'am. Thank you. When I got through talking, I heard the house phone ringing at the desk. By the time I got to it, whoever it was had hung up. It had to be a tenant, of course, and I figured they'd call back."

There was a pause. The tenant could have been Wilma Danay. They both knew it.

Norah went on. "How about the service entrance? Could anyone have got in that way?"

"It's locked at six P.M. weekdays and all day Sundays."

"I notice there's a garage in the building. Is there a connecting door? Could he have come in that way?"

"If he had a key."

Norah turned expectantly to Wyler as he returned.

"According to the night manager of the Pizza Palace, they didn't receive any order from this building at any time today."

And back to Bert Kimmel. "So, somebody bought the pizza and carried it over here and used it as an excuse to get into the building."

"Oh, God . . ."

Between them, Norah Mulcahaney and Simon Wyler got him to a chair. "Are you all right? Would you like a glass of water?"

"Nobody got by me. I swear." He gulped a couple of times. "Could I have a smoke?"

It took four matches before he got the cigarette lit, but Norah waited patiently. "Now, Mr. Kimmel, let's get back to Todd Millard. A boy called 911 and reported a crime in progress. He said somebody was beating his grandmother. That had to be Todd. Now he's gone. Have you any idea where he might be?"

Kimmel choked on the smoke, turned red, tears ran down his raddled cheeks.

"Did you see him leave the building?"

Finally, Kimmel was able to control his coughing. "No, ma'am. I wouldn't have let him go out by himself after dark. I would have stopped him and called upstairs to report to Miss Danay."

"So how could he have got out?"

Kimmel frowned. "He could have taken the elevator down to the basement and gone out the service door."

"But you said that's locked all day Sunday."

"From the outside, not the inside. You can't get in from the street, but you can get out. That's in case of fire." Kimmel hesitated. "He could still be in the building."

Norah pursed her lips. "Thank you, Mr. Kimmel. You've been very helpful. If anything further occurs to you, we'd be grateful if you'd get in touch." As she handed him her card, her mind was already racing ahead.

Why had the perpetrator forced the door of Todd Millard's room? Obviously, because he couldn't get in. But why did he need to get in? How did he know there was anybody inside? Could the boy, hearing the sounds of the struggle, have come out and then, frightened by what he saw, have run back inside? Guesswork, Norah chided herself just as she had Phil Worgan a short while ago. Only one thing was certain: Todd Millard was gone.

Suggesting the child was still in the building was a wild guess, an attempt by the doorman to divert attention from himself, yet she couldn't afford to ignore it. The building consisted of two sections, each twenty-four stories high, occupying half a city block and comprised of two hundred and forty apartments of varying sizes from studios to Wilma Danay's lavish spread of seven rooms. Ringing doorbells after midnight would be futile; no tenant would admit them. She had no search warrant and she could hardly force her way in. If, on the other hand, the child had sought refuge in one of the apartments, the people sheltering him would by now have notified the police. Or should have.

However, the common areas could be searched: main lobby, landings, corridors, stairwells, basement areas such as superintendent's office, boiler room, carpentry shop, tenants' laundry room. It was a maintenance system that could support a small town and did, in fact, service over five hundred people. Norah didn't have the manpower available to do it, so she ordered the building sealed and guards placed at each of the two front entries and the service door. Then she got on the phone to Captain Jacoby. It was three-thirty A.M.

"Sorry to disturb you, Captain."

Jacoby grunted. He liked his full eight hours, but he also demanded to be called when the situation warranted.

"Until we know what's happened to the child, I think we need to keep the lid on this," she concluded her account. "I suggest communication should be by land lines only."

She referred to the public telephone. The reason was to avoid the media cutting in on police radio transmissions. It was one way the word about the assault on Wilma Danay and her death might get out. Once it did, reporters from every service would swarm all over the building. Next, they'd find out about the missing child. That could be fatal.

"Agreed," Manny Jacoby grunted. He might be too rigid sometimes, too bound to go by the book, but he was also fiercely protective of the right of his people to work without interference and second-guessing by outside interests.

Turning out a task force at four A.M. wasn't easy, but Jacoby contacted his executive officer, Art Potts, and ten uniforms reported to Norah within the hour. She divided them into two teams, one headed by Ferdi Arenas, the other by Simon Wyler. While they searched the building, she remained in the Danay apartment and set herself to contacting the parents of the missing child. She settled herself at Wilma Danay's desk in the library and looked through her address book for the numbers she needed. At that hour, Norah fully expected her calls to be answered, but they weren't. None of the persons she tried to reach were where they should have been—in bed and asleep. Not Adele Millard, the boy's mother, but then she was out of town, Norah reminded herself. But what about Richard Millard, the boy's father? Where was he? Only when Norah called Montreal, Canada, did she finally, after several rings, get a response.

"Yolanda Yates?"

"No." The woman sounded as though she'd been wakened, which very likely she had been, but she came quickly alert. Too quickly? As though she'd been expecting a call? "Yolanda isn't here. She left. Who wants her?"

"Is this her sister, Isabel Yates?"

"Yes." The woman was polite but wary. "Who are you?"

"I'm a New York City police officer, Miss Yates, Lieutenant Mulcahaney. Sorry to disturb you at this hour, but I need to contact Yolanda. It's about Wilma Danay."

"Oh, my God!" Isabel Yates exclaimed. "Something's happened, hasn't it? Something bad. Yolanda had a feeling. I tried to talk her out of it, but she wouldn't listen. She insisted on going right back. She took the train. She's on her way. She's due in at Grand Central at about seven-thirty."

"All right. Thank you, Miss Yates."

"Could you tell me what happened? Please."

Norah hedged. "There's been a break-in."

"Oh, my! I'm so sorry. Is she all right? Is Miss Danay all right?"

"I can't say as yet. Are *you* all right, Miss Yates?"

"Me? Oh yes, I am. Sure. Fit as a fiddle."

And she sounded it, too, Norah thought.

"Nothing happened to me, you know. This morning, around noon—I was just back from church—my doorbell rings and there's Yolanda all trembly on the doorstep. She claims a nurse from Montreal General called her in New York and said I'd been in an automobile accident. She came right up. That's natural, eh? Yolanda doesn't fly, so she took the last train from New York Saturday evening and got here Sunday morning. She went straight to the hospital, where nobody knew anything about me or about any accident. I wasn't registered as a patient, and she couldn't find the nurse who had made the call because she forgot to make a note of her name—if the woman ever gave a name." Isabel Yates clucked her disapproval. "So she rushed right over here to the house and here I was as usual and in the pink.

"I told Yolanda she should have talked to me before making the trip. She said she knew that much and she'd asked to talk to me, but the nurse told her I was in a coma. Can you believe that? They must have the wrong name. How could a big hospital make such a mistake?"

Norah didn't point out that since she hadn't been registered as a patient, there was no way the nurse could have gotten the name of her next of kin—right or wrong. "It happens," she said.

"I suppose. At first, Yolanda was relieved. We were glad to see each other. Then she got angry because of what she'd been put through. After that, she began to worry about Miss Danay. So she called. No problem. Miss Danay tried to soothe her. She told Yolanda as long as she was here, she might as well stay and visit awhile. But Yolanda wouldn't hear of it. She was getting more and more nervous. She said something was fishy. Finally, I told her—go back. If she wasn't going to relax and enjoy herself, there was no point in staying. So she left. She took the five-ten and, as I said, she should be walking in or calling . . . No, she won't call," Isabel Yates corrected herself. "Miss Danay sleeps late. Yolanda wouldn't disturb her."

Norah thanked her and hung up.

She made one more try to reach the missing child's parents. Neither of them answered. Norah considered contacting the three bridge players but decided their testimonies could wait till she was able to interrogate them in person. She took another turn around the apartment.

Actually, aside from the broken figurines and the over-turned chairs, everything seemed in place. The paintings hadn't been disturbed; they glowed serenely in their individual spotlights. There were no light patches to indicate any might be missing. Was it possible the intruder hadn't known their value? The Renoir alone had to be worth over a million, maybe two, Norah thought.

In the bedroom, except for the stain on the rug, there was no indication of the death struggle. Jars, bottles, lotions, and powders and perfumes were lined up with precision on the star's dressing table. An antique jewel box was on the bureau. Norah opened it. It was lined in faded blue velvet and the contents arranged with the same regard for order— rings, brooches, necklaces, pearls, diamonds, emeralds. Clearly the purpose of the break-in had not been robbery. Unless . . . It could have been a robbery that Wilma Danay interrupted. The struggle ensued. She plunged a knife into the robber. He struck a blow that killed her and fled without any loot.

First light was breaking and Norah still stood staring at a cluster of tiny droplets of dried blood on the threshold of Todd's room when Arenas and Wyler returned.

"We've gone through all the common areas, from boiler room to broom closet. No trace of the boy," Ferdi reported. "That leaves two hundred and forty apartments."

"And the street," Wyler added. "If he got away."

"We'll proceed on the assumption that he did." Norah's chin was set.

They both knew what that meant.

"Wouldn't he have called his mom or his dad?" Ferdi reasoned.

"He wouldn't have been able to reach them. I've been

sitting here for over an hour myself, trying," Norah told him.

"So why didn't he call 911 again?" Wyler suggested. "He was smart enough to do it the first time."

Norah pointed to the child's clothes neatly laid out on a chair and then the rumpled bed sheets. "He was in his pajamas. He wasn't likely to have any money on him."

"You don't need money to call 911."

"Maybe he didn't know that. He's only a child."

"Sorry, Lieutenant. The thing is, after the perp' killed Miss Danay, you'd expect him to get out fast. But he didn't." The evidence of that—the forced door—was loud in its silence. "Why?"

Clearly a rhetorical question, but before Wyler could supply the answer, the phone on the night stand rang. The gray of dawn was turning to rosy morning yet the sound was somehow sinister. The three stared at the instrument as it rang again. Norah walked over and picked it up.

"Hello?"

"Miss Danay?"

"Who's calling?"

There was a pause.

"I want to speak to Miss Danay. Tell her to come to the phone."

"May I tell her who's calling?"

"You may tell her to come to the phone. Now."

"I'm sorry, she's not available just now. Would you like to leave a message?"

Another pause. Apparently, the caller had not expected difficulty in getting through. "Yeah. All right, I'll leave a message. You tell the big star I have her grandson. If she wants to see the kid again, she better come to the phone. You tell her that."

Norah did some quick thinking. "She can't take your call. She's under sedation. The doctor has put her under sedation. She'll be out for several hours." Would he accept that? She could feel him hesitating. "Is the boy all right?"

"He is for now."

"What do you want? Tell me what you want? I'm her friend. I'll see to it she gets the message as soon as she wakes up."

There was another, longer pause, then without a word, he hung up.

Slowly, Norah did the same. She looked from Arenas to Wyler. The fears she'd tried so hard not to acknowledge could no longer be denied.

"The boy is being held for ransom."

Chapter

FOUR

"Ransom?" Wyler echoed. He stared at Norah Mulcahaney in dismay. "Who does he expect to collect from?"

"From the grandmother, of course. From Wilma Danay."

Arenas gasped. "How can that be?"

"He doesn't know she's dead."

Norah frowned. Now the evidence made sense, she thought. Despite the childish possessions scattered around, the room was without character, like a hotel room. The doorman had said Todd was a frequent visitor, yet not frequent enough for the room to be done over for him. It was significant, Norah thought, that the boy had been snatched from his grandmother's home rather than from his mother's or his father's. So then it was natural that the ransom demand should be made on the grandmother. She was the one who had the money. Homicide could be attributed to a variety of motives, Norah reflected, whereas money was the only motive for kidnapping. Correction: until recently. Lately, divorced parents denied custody were resorting to kidnapping. Whatever the circumstances, it was always an ugly crime and one which often led to murder. In this instance, it had started with murder.

"He doesn't know he killed her." Norah's blue eyes were

dark and somber. "And we'd better make damn sure he doesn't find out. If the perp' learns that Danay isn't around to pay, he could panic and get rid of the boy."

If he hadn't already.

The thought, unspoken, was nevertheless shared. As long as the kidnapper believed there was the possibility of getting paid, he would take reasonable care of the child. Instinct had warned her not to let the story out, and thank God for that.

Norah had looked forward to going home for a couple of hours at least to shower and change and get a bite of breakfast before meeting the companion, Yolanda Yates, on her return from Montreal. That was now out of the question. She had told the caller that Wilma Danay was under sedation and would not wake for several hours. His timetable had been disrupted and a third party introduced—Norah, in the guise of a friend of the star's. He would need to factor that in. It might be late afternoon before he made contact again, or it could happen within the hour.

So she would start the investigation right from here, using the library as a temporary office. She could lay out the agenda, make the assignments, all according to routine— except that the case was anything but routine. Wilma Danay's death had not even been officially designated a homicide. And suppose, while she was on the phone, the kidnapper called and got a busy signal? What would he think? Naturally, that the police were there.

"We need another line," she told Wyler. Get the telephone company to install it. Right away."

The primary thrust of the investigation shifted from finding a killer to preserving the life of a child.

It meant waking Captain Jacoby for the second time that night.

"I can't call from here and I can't leave. Explain to the captain," she charged Ferdi.

She would never have given such an assignment to anyone else. Though Ferdi was ten years younger and she outranked him, they were friends. They understood each other. They were *simpatico*; Joe's word. Ferdi had seen his fiancée, a policewoman on decoy duty, killed before his eyes and had been helpless to do anything about it. Norah supported him during a long bout of grief and depression. When she lost Joe, Ferdi had comforted her. They shared the same standards, the same work ethic. They had watched the deterioration of the city, the chaos on the streets, and the growing inability of the force to deal with it.

"Sorry to lay this on you, Ferdi."

Norah smiled and he smiled back, thinking that she had suffered twice and that the signs of the second loss were visible, at least to those who knew her. It was not the few threads of gray in her hair, nor the new lines on her brow, but rather that her spirit was not the same. He missed Norah's verve and her enthusiasm for the work; the energy of commitment.

"No problem," he assured her and started for the door.

"On the way, check that there are no uniforms anywhere in the building or around it. Make sure."

"Right."

"If it's absolutely necessary, you can get me on the house phone, but remember the call will be monitored." There was no need to remind him; that she did so, indicated how tense she was.

Ferdi nodded, and this time she let him go.

The crime-scene detectives had long since finished, the hastily assembled search force disbanded, and now finally Norah was alone. Since the party, she'd been going full speed mentally and physically. The abrupt cessation of activity left her at a temporary loss. She returned to the library.

The room faced north and was still only in a gray halflight. A single flip of the wall switch turned the on desk lamp and a lamp on a long table in front of a wall of books. Nothing in here had been disturbed. It was quiet and restful. Norah took off her uniform jacket, draped it over the back of the leather-upholstered desk chair, and sat down. Propping her elbows on the desk, she rested her head in her hands and closed her eyes. The next thing she knew the doorbell was ringing. It was the installer from the telephone company.

As he was finishing, Manny Jacoby arrived. She hadn't expected him to come in person. She wondered what Ferdi had said.

"Sorry to disturb you again, Captain."

"You did right."

Jacoby's round face was more puffy than usual; his small eyes bleary; he hadn't bothered to shave—he'd do that later when he got to his office—but he wore a regular business suit with a fresh white shirt and his tie was carefully knotted. He took a quick look around the apartment without missing a thing—neither the valuable paintings and furniture, nor the indications of the violent struggle. He walked past the broken door of the missing boy's bedroom and stood at the chalk outline indicating where the body of Wilma Danay had lain.

"She was a mysterious woman. She was an enigma; you could see in her whatever you wanted to see." Jacoby spoke softly. "That was her appeal. She offered the fulfillment of every man's desire." After a long moment of silence, he turned away.

First Phil Worgan and now Manny Jacoby, Norah thought. The woman must have had some kind of magic. She followed the captain back along the corridor to the library.

"I'm Captain Jacoby," he told the installer. "When can we use the phone?"

"Right now, Captain."

Jacoby picked up the receiver, dialed, and after a short wait nodded, indicating the line was ringing and the installer could go. "Dr. Worgan? Manny Jacoby. We need to know the cause of death. I know it's early, but it's a matter of jurisdiction."

He was referring to the FBI, of course, Norah realized. They had to be informed. It had been at the back of her mind. They might or might not want to enter the case actively or elect to stay in the background. It would depend on a lot of things.

"I understand, but I don't think that needs to concern us. I think we can go ahead and investigate it as a homicide. Thanks, Doc." He hung up.

"Doc says the victim took a heavy beating. One of the blows knocked her off her feet and sent her reeling to crack her head against a wall. Another fractured her jaw."

Norah's blue eyes blazed.

"But death was due to heart failure."

"Heart failure," Norah repeated.

"She had a heart condition. And she wasn't exactly young," Jacoby pointed out.

"No," Norah agreed. "That explains why the perp' doesn't know she's dead. But the heart attack was brought on by shock and *he's* responsible. It's death occurring during the commission of a felony."

"No argument from me." Jacoby passed a hand over his mouth in a gesture indicating he was still assessing the situation.

"He doesn't know he killed her," Norah repeated. "And the longer we can keep him from finding out . . ."

"Yes," Manny Jacoby nodded. "We'll let it ride as far as the FBI is concerned. For now."

While Manny Jacoby was not one to shirk responsibility, neither did he seek it out. He had reached his present rank by scoring high on the civil-service exam, establishing discipline and control within his command, and by adhering to the venerable army precept—never volunteer. Maybe he realized that he had risen as far as he could by that route and that to make it to a higher post some risk was necessary.

What worried Norah was her own ability to deal with the situation. Early in her marriage when it became apparent she would not conceive, she and Joe adopted a four-year-old boy, Mark. His natural mother had turned up and attempted to use him as a bargaining chip to suppress evidence in an old murder case. There had not been even a fleeting thought of turning the evidence over, but as long as they refused, the child would be in danger. And even if they gave in, there would be other occasions; they would be subject to other threats. In the end, the only way to protect Mark was to turn him back to the adoption agency. Norah would never forget the look on Mark's face when she handed him over. Never. It had been a terrible decision. It had come close to destroying the marriage.

"I've been trying to contact Mrs. Millard or the professor, but so far . . ." Norah stopped. She looked to see if Jacoby, too, had caught the sound of the front door opening. He had. Together, they moved quietly toward the foyer.

A woman had just let herself in. She was tall and big-boned but thin. Her frizzed blonde hair was at odds with her gaunt features. Her heavy makeup didn't help. She wore a tailored gray suit with a frilly lace blouse and red sandals. She carried a small overnight bag. Jacoby nudged Norah and the two of them moved out of the shadows.

"Miss Yates?" Norah asked.

The woman jumped. "Who are you? What are you doing here?"

"Police. Don't be afraid. This is Captain Jacoby. I'm Lieutenant Mulcahaney."

Yolanda Yates turned the color of putty. She took in the overturned chairs and the shattered china. "What's happened? Where's Wilma? Where's Miss Danay?"

"I'm afraid I have bad news, Ms. Yates. Let's sit down." Gently placing her hand on the woman's elbow, Norah led her to a small settee well off to the side of the formal salon from where she couldn't see into the bedroom wing.

Norah sat beside her. Manny Jacoby pulled up a chair but left it to Norah to conduct the interview.

"Someone broke in during the night, possibly with robbery in mind," Norah explained. "It looks like Miss Danay came on the intruder. There was a struggle. He was too much for her."

Yolanda Yates stared at Norah. "You mean . . . You can't mean . . . ?"

"I'm sorry, Miss Yates. I'm very sorry."

"It can't be. My God, no . . ." The tears brimmed and spilled down her haggard cheeks. "I knew something was wrong. I just knew it. I sensed it. Where is she? I want to see her."

"That's not possible right now. I'm sorry. But if you feel up to it, we'd appreciate your answering a few questions. Could you do that, Miss Yates?"

"I'll try."

"Thank you. Would you like anything—coffee? Some water?" Yolanda Yates shook her head. "Well then, let's start at the beginning. How long have you known Miss Danay?"

"I went to work for Wilma Danay after her first big hit, *Desert Love*. She needed someone to answer her fan mail. Soon, there was too much of it for me to handle alone. We hired an assistant and then a staff. I was in charge and I also took care of her personal correspondence and ran her household—paid the rent, utilities, the cook, the maid, the chauffeur, and so on. We became friends. That was about the time she married her second husband, Quentin Noble. You remember him?"

"I've heard of him."

"Wonderful, brilliant man." Yolanda Yates's eyes had a faraway look. "A superb actor and director. He taught Wilma. He molded her. Made her a star like none before or after. When Quentin Noble died in the automobile crash, Wilma was devastated. She went into seclusion for months. She asked me to move in and live with her, and I've been with her ever since. That's over twenty years."

"Wasn't another woman involved in the crash? I seem to have read somewhere that Wilma and Quentin were on the verge of separating."

"There was a young actress in the car," Yates replied, "but there was nothing going on between her and Quentin. He was just giving her a lift from the studio. There are always people ready to think the worst."

Norah knew about that. When Randall died, people who had called themselves his friends were ready to believe every unfounded accusation. "Didn't Miss Danay marry again, a third time?"

"Yes, that's right," the secretary-companion replied. "She married Peter Bouchard, but it didn't work. It was like coming back to earth after living with the angels. From the sublime to the pedestrian. They tried a couple of films together—three, to be exact. All flops at the box office."

"So she retired," Norah concluded.

"She wanted to be remembered at her peak."

"Some say she had no choice, that nobody wanted to sink any more money in Wilma Danay. They say she couldn't perform without Noble. That she was a Trilby who had lost her Svengali."

Yolanda Yates merely shook her head.

"Peter Bouchard was here last night playing bridge," Norah observed.

"Yes. They're still good friends."

"And Mrs. Bouchard, the current wife. She and Miss Danay are also friends?"

"Good friends. Why not?"

"I couldn't say." Norah opened out her hands, palms up, for emphasis. Where love had once been, how could you substitute friendship? It depended, she supposed, on the original intensity and quality of the emotion. "What about the rest of Miss Danay's family? There's a daughter, I'm told. By which husband?"

"The first, Frank Grillo. Frank married Wilma when she was sixteen. Smart man. Smart enough to see Wilma's potential and develop it. Smart enough to know when he had reached his limit in what he could do for her and let her go to Quentin Noble. He did continue as her agent and handled her investments till his death six years ago. He died in his sleep." She paused, perhaps thinking how differently the end had come for Wilma Danay. Tears welled in her tired eyes.

"She must have had some enemies," Norah continued. "Nobody goes through life without hurting feelings, especially, I would think, in the theatrical world. Emotions are so close to the surface."

"That's exactly right, Lieutenant. Artists don't hold back their feelings, don't let them fester. They get rid of the antagonism, let it out, and then it's done with and forgotten."

"So it's your opinion there was no personal link between whoever broke in here and Miss Danay?"

"I can't imagine what it might be."

She hadn't mentioned the boy, Norah thought, casting a sideways glance at Manny Jacoby. The companion hadn't said a word about Todd. "You did know that Miss Danay's grandson was staying with her over the weekend?" she asked.

"Yes." Yolanda Yates swallowed. "Why? He's all right, isn't he?"

Norah got up and motioned for Yates to follow. She led the way to the bedroom corridor and the open door of Todd's room. She pointed to the lock. "It's been forced, as you can see."

The companion advanced only far enough to see there was no one there. "What's happened to Todd? Where is he?"

Now Norah took her across the way to the master bedroom. For a moment it appeared as though Yolanda Yates would not cross that threshold either. But then, without any urging from Norah or Manny Jacoby, yet in evident fear of what she would find, she did go in. She stopped short at the chalk outline of the body. She began to heave, turned, and ran for the bathroom. After a few minutes, the retching stopped. There was the sound of running water. It was turned off. Another short while, and she was back.

"Are you all right?" Norah asked.

The woman nodded. "What happened to Todd? Where is he? Wilma loved that boy. She loved him more than anything in the world. She would have done anything for him."

She did, Norah thought; she gave her life.

Chapter_____
_____FIVE

At seven-thirty Monday morning, Adele Millard stood at the threshold of the main dining room of the Drake Hotel and prepared to make her entrance.

It was filled with business people, mostly men, though there was a scattered handful of women. A low murmur of conversation, accompanied by the clink of fine china and crystal, matched the dignity of the room and indicated these were not casual tourists preparing to start on a day of shopping and sightseeing. This was the hour of the power breakfast. Every table represented a high-level meeting. There, avoiding ringing telephones, distracting interruptions, the deals were made and the policies set. Holding herself proudly erect, Ms. Millard followed the maitre d' to the table where her new partners waited. She walked with poise and confidence.

Last night had been a big night, a night for celebrating; a night to remember. She had drunk more champagne than she should have and it had left her with a pounding headache, but she showed no trace of discomfort. She wore a severely tailored navy blue suit with a narrow band of white edging at the collar. The diamond and pearl brooch, a wedding gift from her mother and the only piece of jewelry she hadn't either sold or pawned, was discreet and at the same time impressive. She wore her chestnut hair pulled back to show off her classic profile and flawless skin, a style affected by Wilma Danny at the height of her fame. The star had possessed a luminous glow that her daughter did not, and the severity of the style that had served to intensify the mother's beauty revealed discontent amounting to sullenness in the daughter. Not this morning, however, not at this moment. Adele Millard had reached the first of the goals she had set herself and temporarily, at least, she was satisfied. Her dark eyes sparkled as she reached the table and the two men waiting for her rose from their seats.

"Good morning, Adele," John Prescott said, and Wilfred Hammer echoed as the maitre d' seated her and withdrew.

She looked around, but no one was paying any attention to her. That was now, she thought; the time would come when she would be recognized, when there would be a buzz as word of who she was passed from table to table and all eyes would be on her. It would not be the mindless admiration of movie fans, but the respect of the movers and shakers. Adele had no talent for acting—posturing and mimicking to her mind—and she wasn't interested in it. She had a flair for salesmanship; she could promote and sell just about anything. A talent inherited from her father. Last night the contract making her a partner in the small but prestigious advertising firm of Hammer, Prescott—and now, Millard—had been signed in an aura of mutual satisfaction. The three signatories had each gained something and that was the basis for a good relationship. Adele Millard brought her talent and she also brought a considerable investment.

Both men looked at her closely as they seated themselves again. They had noted with disapproval that she had drunk deeply last night. They were scheduled to meet the new client in two hours. She, having laid out the campaign and made the initial contact, was scheduled also to make the presentation.

"Sleep well?" Wilfred Hammer asked.

"Like a baby," she lied.

It was not generally known that Hammer, Prescott was experiencing financial difficulty. While they tried to make a virtue out of a small stable of clients, the truth was they were aggressively seeking new accounts. Their fame was based on an innovative approach that resulted in high product identification, but their last success was too many years in the past. They needed fresh blood and a new outlook. They also needed an infusion of money. But money alone would not have brought entry. Investment wasn't that hard to find, nor talent. It was the combination that Adele Millard offered plus control of an internationally known star willing to sacrifice art for commerce.

As one waiter appeared to pour the coffee, another came carrying a telephone.

"Call for Ms. Millard."

She took the instrument and as she listened Adele Millard's expression changed. "Do whatever is necessary. Pay whatever he wants. I'll get there as fast as I can." She pushed the antenna down but sat staring straight ahead without moving.

"Adele?" Wilfred Hammer, the senior of the partners and the one who had first favored bringing Adele Millard into the firm, leaned forward to try to read her expression. "What's happened?"

"That was the police. In New York. My child, my son, is missing. There's a possibility he's been kidnapped."

Both men gaped.

"I have to go back right away."

"Yes, of course," Prescott said. Having been doubtful initially about Millard's qualifications, he was now convinced and eager to have her succeed.

"I'm sorry about the meeting this morning. Explain to the client. Ask for a postponement. Or maybe you could make the presentation yourselves . . ."

"We'll arrange everything, don't worry," Prescott assured her and Hammer nodded. In those first moments their concern was all for her.

"Can we help? Is there anything we can do? Anything at all?"

"If you could help me get on the first plane out?"

"You'll be out within the hour," Hammer promised. "How about money? Has the kidnapper made a demand yet?"

"The officer didn't say."

"If you need money . . ."

The partnership contract had been signed, but she had not yet turned over the money.

"As far as we're concerned we can wait. There's no urgency."

The fact was that the contract specified a time limit for payment. They were all aware of it.

"I can get a loan from the bank," she told them. "I'll manage." She got up. "I have to go now."

She made her way between the tables with her new partners trailing behind her.

The phone was ringing as Richard Millard pulled into the driveway. It rang insistently. Millard heard it but he didn't hurry. Anyone calling before eight in the morning had urgent business and would call again. Probably had already called several times. He turned off the ignition, got out, and went around to the other side to help his pregnant wife.

Professor Richard Millard was a big man, overweight but well-proportioned so that he gave the impression of being solid rather than fat. His hair was still thick, blond, and only streaked with silver. A heavy beard camouflaged the weakness of his chin. He carried a pipe that was seldom lit and habitually wore one or another of his wardrobe of Harris tweed jackets. He projected the image of an easygoing, affable, and understanding teacher and family man. The opposite was true. He was demanding in both roles, but he rewarded those who met his standards. The bright, hardworking student would receive encouragement and help. His new wife, having fulfilled his dearest wish by becoming pregnant almost immediately after their marriage, was treated with loving care.

"Are you sure you don't want to go to the hospital?" he pressed as she got out of the car, awkwardly balancing herself and the child in her belly.

"I'm sure. Please, Richard, don't fuss."

Going away had been her idea. Coming back so soon, his.

The baby was due in a couple of weeks. After he came—the tests indicated it would be a boy—the baby would demand and need all of her attention. So she had suggested they get away for a few days alone. It was to be an idyll they could look back on later when nerves would be frayed by a baby's crying and sleep interrupted by night feedings. It was to serve as a remembrance and a promise. Richard had agreed, and to guard against interruption had left no forwarding address or telephone number, going so far as to disconnect the answering machine. He had chosen Montauk at the tip of Long Island. It was near enough for a comfortable drive, and being out of season the rates would be low. Staying into the early part of the week ensured additional savings.

Everything started off well. They arrived on Friday in time for a good shore dinner. On Saturday morning they got up early, strolled along the beach. In the afternoon, the rain began. From a gentle drizzle it progressed by evening into a howling nor'easter. They couldn't go out in it. Inside, there was nothing to do but sit in the lobby and stare at the tormented ocean and listen to the distant dismal groan of the foghorn.

Richard paced. He hadn't brought anything to read; he hadn't brought the manuscript he was working on. He hadn't expected to have time for either.

Louise didn't mind the inactivity. There was no housework, no meals to prepare. She dozed in her chair till Richard irritably announced it was time to turn in.

By Sunday morning the storm was gone and the sky cleared, but it was cold and windy and Richard remained surly. "How do you feel?" he kept asking and was not particularly pleased nor relieved by Louise's assurance that she was fine.

The day dragged on to early cocktails.

"It was a mistake to come," he grumbled. "I shouldn't have let you talk me into it. It's too close to your time. Suppose you go into labor way out here in the middle of nowhere? If anything should happen to the baby or to you, I'd never forgive myself."

At last Louise understood what he wanted, but the suggestion or request must come from her. "Maybe we should go home."

"Well, if that's what you want. If you'd feel more comfortable at home . . ."

"I guess I would feel more comfortable at home. Yes."

He was instantly, eagerly energetic. "If that's what you want, then we'll go home."

She had thought that would mean leaving Monday morning, but having extracted the decision from her, Richard couldn't wait, not even for dinner. "We'll grab a bite on route. If we're going, the sooner the better." He packed, helped Louise pack, paid the bill, loaded the car. Neither of the ferries connecting Long Island to Connecticut was in operation, so they had to take the long way back, as they had coming out, only this time Richard didn't complain. He was an intense driver; he kept his foot steady on the accelerator and concentrated on his destination. They should have been home before midnight, but a flat just past Riverhead caused them to pull off at the shoulder. As Richard finished changing the tire, an unpredicted downpour accompanied by terrifying sky-to-ground lightning left them in a mudhole. He had to go for help. Surprisingly, he took it all without complaint. Louise didn't complain, either; what would have been the use?

Now at last they were home.

"I can run you right over to the hospital, if you say the word."

But for Louise it was finally too much. "For God's sake, Richard, no!" she snapped. "I just want my own bed. I just want to crawl between the covers in my own bed. It was a terrible, awful trip. We should have waited till morning."

It wasn't like Louise Millard to criticize her husband, justified or not.

She was half his age and four years younger than his first wife. They had both been Millard's students. Where Adele was dark, sultry, commanding, Louise was pretty and pert. She had short blonde hair, neat features, blue eyes. She believed she understood the man she'd married and what he wanted and needed. She was eager to provide it, to conform to his requirements, whereas Adele had insisted on her own way. Louise intended to support rather than challenge. She was very sure of herself and certain she would succeed where Adele had failed. From what Richard had told her and others, too, Adele constantly found fault, was dissatisfied with her lot, had come close to being a shrew. Louise had promised herself never to fall into that trap. So now she apologized as soon as the words were spoken.

"I'm sorry, Richard. I didn't mean to put the blame on you. The whole thing was my idea; it's my fault. I'm just so tired."

"Darling, of course. I understand. Not another word." He put his arm around her and helped her the two steps up to the front door and helped her inside.

The phone started ringing again.

He ignored it. "I don't think you should climb the stairs. Why don't you use the spare room for now?"

"No, I want my own bed."

He suppressed a sigh. "At least rest fifteen or twenty minutes before going up."

The phone had rung at least three times and Richard Millard continued to ignore it.

"Aren't you going to answer?"

"It can wait till you're settled."

She sat on the hall bench. "Answer it, Richard."

He shrugged, walked over to the small stand under the stair. "Hello? Yes, this is Professor Millard. Who's calling?" By his tone he indicated displeasure at being disturbed, but as he listened his attitude changed. "Have you notified Mrs. Millard? . . . Oh, all right. Good. Where should I go—to her place? . . . Oh, Miss Danay's. All right, thank you . . . Yes, I'm leaving right away." He hung up, looking dazed.

"Todd's been kidnapped. That was the police."

"What?"

"He was staying with Wilma for the weekend. There was a break-in and he's disappeared. The kidnapper has already made contact."

Kidnapped! Louise Millard thought. Shock was followed by disbelief. *Things like this don't happen to people like us.* "What does he want?"

"Money. What else?"

She had never seen Richard look so helpless. He loved his

son. The only real regret he had over the divorce was the loss of Todd. He had fought for custody. He had depleted his resources in lawyer's fees. But the ruling had been in the mother's favor, as it usually was. Nevertheless, he was deeply disappointed. The visitation rights were liberal, yet he was constantly asking Adele for additional time with the boy. At first, Adele had refused, rigidly and unrelentingly. If she no longer cared for Richard, why did she derive satisfaction from hurting him? Louise wondered. After she and Richard were married, Adele softened a bit and allowed the boy to spend more time with his father. Probably she thought the presence of the child would cause awkwardness in the honeymoon household, would be a reminder to the ex-husband and his new wife. Since Adele was the one who had walked out, who had wanted the divorce, why should she resent Richard's happiness in his second marriage? She was just that kind of woman, Louise thought.

For herself, Louise liked Todd. He was bright, alert; a sturdy, healthy child. He was wise beyond his years and seemed to understand the situation between his parents and accept it. He was polite, evinced no resentment toward his father's second wife, and treated Louise as someone between aunt and friend. He accepted her help with his homework; had seemed to enjoy their outings—skating at a nearby rink, museum trips. If it weren't that he was a constant reminder of Adele, Louise would have welcomed his visits, could have clasped him to her heart. Now, with her own child about to be born, Todd was not the threat he had been. Poor Todd, Louise thought with a sudden pang, what a terrible thing to go through. How frightened he must be. She hoped he hadn't been hurt. A terrible dread seized her and the sweat broke out all over her body.

"We have no money," she said.

"Wilma will pay. Naturally."

"Oh." Louise nodded, relieved and also ashamed that she had thought of their own needs first.

"I'm driving in. Will you be all right?"

"Of course. Is Adele there?"

"They contacted her in Chicago. She's on her way."

"I'll come with you."

"It's not necessary."

"I want to be with you."

"There's nothing you can do," Millard explained patiently but with an edge. "You'll only complicate matters. You've had a rough night. If you should go into premature labor . . . For God's sake, stop being jealous of Adele and use your head."

"I'm not jealous!" But she was. "I'm sorry."

"Don't be sorry. Just make sure our baby is normal and healthy."

She reached up and twined her arms around his neck and pressed her belly with its precious burden against him. "I'll call Carrie to come over and stay with me in case I need to get to the hospital."

"That's more like it. That's my sensible girl."

She watched him leave. She stood at the window and watched as he got into the car and backed out of the driveway. She returned his wave cheerily. Then when he was gone, she let the tears come.

Chapter
SIX

With both parents finally contacted and on the way, Norah urged Yolanda Yates to go to her room and rest.

"Suppose the . . . person who has Todd . . . calls again?"

"I'll be here, Miss Yates. I've already spoken to him; he won't be surprised to hear my voice. He'll deal with me." She wished she felt as sure as she tried to sound.

"There'll be someone here at all times," Captain Jacoby assured the companion. When she was gone, he turned to Norah. "And you can't go without sleep indefinitely. The tough part is yet to come; you know that. I'll send someone to relieve you."

"I can't leave. I've got to be the one who answers the phone. I've got to stay at least till the mother shows up."

"I'm not telling you to leave, just to stretch out and grab a little shut-eye."

"Captain, once I close my eyes, I'll be dead to the world. I may not hear the phone."

"I'll send someone to stay with you and make sure you hear it. You're not superwoman, Lieutenant. When are you going to accept that?"

And suddenly, with the sun well up and both parents notified and on their way, with nothing that couldn't wait, weariness enveloped Norah. She went to the library and lay down on the couch as Captain Jacoby had suggested, but she resisted closing her eyes. If it were only a matter of Wilma Danay's murder, she would have welcomed sleep, but there were two victims in this case and one of them was still living. At least, she hoped so. Norah said a silent prayer that Todd Millard had managed to survive and that somehow they would get him back. Deep in thought, Norah was startled by the ring not of the phone but of the doorbell. Whoever the captain had sent, he hadn't wasted any time. She looked through the peephole.

"Kathryn!"

She pulled the door open.

Kathryn Webber, in uniform and carrying a small canvas duffle bag that looked very much like one Norah owned, stood on the threshold. She was smiling broadly. "Good morning, Lieutenant. I brought you some things from your apartment—a change of clothes, toothbrush, makeup, like that. I thought you could probably use them."

Momentarily speechless, Norah stepped to one side to let the girl in.

"Did the captain tell you to go to my apartment?"

"No, not exactly." Kathryn was taken aback by Norah's evident displeasure.

"You took it on yourself?"

"Well, I happened to overhear him tell Detective Neel that you were here and that you'd been here all night."

"You eavesdropped."

"No. They were talking in the hall. I passed by. I couldn't help but hear. Nobody could."

"The captain didn't send you here, did he?"

Kathryn hesitated. "No, ma'am."

Norah was shocked. "You took the whole thing on yourself: first, to go to my place. By the way, how did you get into my apartment?"

"The super let me in. I told him who I was and what I was after." She lowered her eyes. "I said you'd sent me."

"And then I suppose you came straight over here and told the doorman I was up here waiting for you?"

Kathryn Webber nodded, by now much chastened.

"Are you aware that we don't want anybody to know the police are up here?"

She blushed. "No, ma'am. I'm sorry. I thought you'd be needing these, that's all." She thrust the satchel at Norah. "I thought you wouldn't want a man going through your things."

Norah took a deep breath. "Next time you have an idea or a suggestion, go to your sergeant." She took the bag. "Thank you."

Kathryn Webber brightened instantly. "Would you like me to stay awhile?"

Was it possible the girl honestly didn't understand she was out of line? Norah wondered. If so, she had no idea how to get through to her. "No, thank you. Somebody is on the way." And just then the doorbell rang. "I'll get it."

This time it was Detective Danny Neel. His grin was big and easy. "Morning, Lieut'." Spotting Kathryn right behind Norah, he smiled at her, too.

"This is Officer Webber," Norah said. "She lives in the area and she was kind enough to go over to my place and pick up some personal things for me." She indicated the duffle bag.

Detective Second Grade Daniel Neel was a stocky, strong "broth of a lad" with black curly hair and dark eyes, and a perfect set of white teeth that he liked to show off along with the dimple at the right side of his chin. He had been working for Norah Mulcahaney for over a year and he didn't understand why the lieutenant was taking the trouble to explain.

Norah didn't know why she was, either. "So, thanks again, Officer Webber."

It was clear dismissal, yet Webber was hanging back. "Anything else I can do for you, Lieutenant?"

"You've done more than enough."

Webber bowed her head and let herself out.

Was he missing something? Neel wondered, then shrugged. "I brought coffee and Danish."

"Great. I can sure use it."

They went back to the library and after the snack, Norah took off her shoes, lay down on the couch, and fell asleep just about instantly.

The next thing she knew, Neel was shaking her gently.

"Lieutenant, Mrs. Millard is here."

She awoke fully oriented. She sat up, put on her shoes, tucked her shirt in, and entered the foyer just as Adele Millard was dismissing the porter who had brought up her luggage.

Adele Millard's face was drawn, soot and grime and sweat ground into the lines and furrows. The navy suit that had looked so fresh and trim at the power breakfast hours ago was rumpled and soiled; the white edging at the neckline stained. Adele Millard looked what she was—travel-worn, weary, deeply anxious. She bore a striking resemblance to Wilma Danay, Norah thought.

"Are you the officer I spoke to on the telephone?"

"I'm Norah Mulcahaney, yes."

After one swift appraising glance Adele Millard's eyes swept on to the open archway and the living room. She caught her breath. "What happened here? Where's my mother?"

"I'm sorry, Mrs. Millard. It seemed best not to tell you over the telephone. Perhaps you'd like to sit down."

"Just tell me—where's my mother?"

Norah made it as simple and brief as possible. There would be time later for details. "There was a break-in. The purpose could have been either robbery or kidnapping; we're not sure. Either way, your mother interrupted. There was a struggle." No matter how many times she went through it, it was never easy to break the news and never would be. The best way was to say it straight out. "Your mother had a heart attack. I'm so very, very sorry."

Adele Millard put her hands over her face. She swayed slightly but maintained her balance. After a few moments, she dropped her hands.

"Where is she? Where's my mother *now*."

"At the morgue."

"No! My God, you can't do that. I won't allow it."

"It's done, Mrs. Millard. I'm sorry, but it's the law. We had to establish the cause of death."

"My poor mother. Oh, my poor mother. You didn't . . . ?"

"Touch her face? No, of course not."

Adele Millard nodded and sat down. "You said there was a ransom demand?"

"Yes. A man called. He wanted to speak to Miss Danay. I took the call and pretended to be a friend. I told him Miss Danay was ill and under sedation. He said he would call back and if she wanted to see her grandson again, she had better speak to him."

"He doesn't know?"

"Apparently not."

The woman shook her head in dismay. She indicated a black lacquer cabinet adorned with golden dragons. "There's sherry in there. If I could have a glass, please?"

At Norah's nod, Danny Neel went over, selected a glass from the array, poured, and brought it over. Adele Millard drank slowly but without stopping till she had finished. She set the empty glass down firmly but didn't ask for another.

"What happens when he calls back? Will he call back?"

"Oh, yes, he will." I hope he will, Norah amended silently.

"What should we do? How should we respond?"

Norah had given it a lot of thought. "He'll insist on speaking with Miss Danay of course. He won't accept excuses and he won't deal with intermediaries. Hopefully, he will deal with you."

"Suppose he doesn't?"

"If he wants to collect . . ."

Adele Millard scowled. "I have no money. He must know that."

There was no question about that, Norah thought; it was why he had chosen to make the demand on the grandmother.

"Are you your mother's heir?"

"Yes, I suppose I am. But I don't think there's much ready cash available. Her assets were mostly in these." She indicated the paintings and furnishings. "It would take time to sell something and realize cash. He won't wait. How can he afford to wait?" Her question ended in a wail of despair as her control broke.

Norah went over and sat beside her. Her instinct was to put an arm around her as she wept for a double loss—her mother and her son, but Norah held back; she sensed that despite her grief, Adele Millard would not accept the comfort of a stranger.

"What will happen to Todd?"

"Todd is all right," Norah assured her. "He'll continue to be all right as long as the kidnapper thinks he's going to get his ransom. It's up to you to convince him that you're willing to pay."

"I am. I am."

"And that you can get the money. He'll assume you're going to get it from your mother."

"But she's dead."

"Remember that he doesn't know that. He probably thinks he knocked her out, but she was still alive when he left. It could be true. The heart attack could have come later."

"But he's responsible!"

"Of course. But for now we have to set that aspect of the case to one side. We don't want to frighten him or make it any more difficult for him than we have to. We want to encourage him to turn over the boy. Okay, Mrs. Millard?"

"I understand. Only I don't know where I'm going to get the money. Maybe the bank would give me a loan? With all this for collateral, they should, don't you think?" She made a sweeping gesture that encompassed all the treasures around them. "That's going to take time though, plus which these things don't really belong to me, not till the will is probated." She kept raising objections and then trying to meet them.

"Maybe you could borrow from friends? How about Todd's father?" Norah suggested.

"Has he been told?"

"Yes. He's on his way."

Adele Millard sighed. "Richard has no money, either. Not this kind of money."

"Addie! Oh, Addie!"

Yolanda Yates, wearing a green plaid flannel robe with the hem of a pink nightgown showing, burst into the room holding her arms widely outstretched. She advanced on Adele Millard and enfolded her. "My dear child. My poor baby. I'm so sorry. Darling, I'm so very sorry."

Hitherto self-possessed, the young woman gave in to her sorrow. She rested her head against the companion's bosom, moaning. "What happened? Where were you, Yolanda? You should have been here. Why weren't you here?"

"I was in Montreal. I got word that Isabel had been in an automobile accident, so I dropped everything and went. It wasn't true. I got up there and she was fine. Nothing had happened at all. It was a mistake. I came back as fast as I could." She paused. "You know I loved Wilma. I really did."

The roles reversed and Adele Millard became the comforter. She raised her head, looked deep into the older woman's eyes and kissed her. "We both loved her."

"It's clear that the person who planned this knew Miss Danay and was familiar with her living arrangements," Norah told them. "He knew Mrs. Millard would be out of town over the long weekend and would leave her son with his grandmother. He lured Ms. Yates away with a lie. With the coast clear, he thought he'd have an easy time of it; an eighty-four-year-old woman and a ten-year-old boy shouldn't have been any trouble. But he hadn't counted on Miss Danay's resistance or the boy's courage and resourcefulness. While his grandmother struggled with the intruder, Todd called 911."

"You're saying that somebody we know, somebody close, a friend—someone we think of as a friend—did this?"

"Set it up anyway."

"What should we do? What's next?"

"I think it's time to call the FBI."

At that the full impact of the situation hit her. The blood drained out of Adele Millard's face. "Do we have to?"

"They're the experts," Norah said. "They know what to do. They've done it hundreds of times before."

"And how many times have they got the child back?"

"With them, you've got a chance. Without them, less of a chance."

"They go after the criminal, I could care less about the criminal. I want my son back."

"No one can promise you that."

"I know. I know." Abruptly, Adele Millard got up and strode to the window. She looked out and saw nothing of the fresh, bright morning. "I don't want the FBI," she said finally. Then she turned to face Norah directly. "You've already talked to the kidnapper, so you can stay. Nobody else. Nobody."

"I can't take that responsibility."

It was a blow, unexpected, and Mrs. Millard winced. "You mean you won't."

"I mean, I don't have the right."

"I thought it was your job."

"I'm a police officer. I have to follow the rules."

"Fine. You do that. You know, when we talked on the telephone early this morning, I sensed an empathy. I felt that you cared, really cared, that you would help me get my son back. But I see I was wrong. I don't suppose you have children of your own, Lieutenant?"

"It isn't a matter of having or not having children, or of caring. I do care, believe me. It's a question of procedure, of following a tested pattern that has proved effective."

The two women faced each other. The ring of the telephone in the library jolted them both.

"I'll get it." Mrs. Millard strode past Norah and after a second's hesitation, she followed and so did Yolanda Yates.

With a shaking hand, Mrs. Millard picked up the receiver. "Hello?"

No answer. Despite the silence, however, the line was very much alive; she could sense it. "Hello? Hello?" Silently, she exhorted, *Don't hang up. Oh, please God, don't let him hang up.*

"Who's this?" A man's voice.

"I'm Adele Millard. Todd's mother. Do you have my boy? Is he all right?"

"I want to talk to Wilma Danay."

"She can't come to the phone."

"You've got thirty seconds to get Wilma Danay to the telephone or I hang up and you never hear from me or see your son again."

Chapter
SEVEN

Adele Millard put her hand over the mouthpiece. "He insists on talking to my mother." Her eyes, fixed on Norah Mulcahaney, were desperate.

Norah thought fast then mouthed the words: *Heart attack. Coma. Tell him.*

"My mother's had a heart attack. She's in a coma. I don't know, there's no way of knowing, when she'll come out of it. I want my son back. Please, tell me what you want. Tell me what to do. I'll do anything. Give you anything. Please."

There was a short pause, then the man, his voice deep and rasping, replied, "I want five hundred thousand dollars in unmarked bills. I'll call at three this afternoon. Be ready to deliver."

"I can't," she blurted instinctively. "It's too soon. I can't raise that kind of money so fast. I need more time."

But he had already hung up.

Adele Millard let the receiver clatter into its cradle. "He wants five hundred thousand by three this afternoon. It's impossible. I can't raise the money, not in that time, anyway."

"You might be as well off refusing to pay," Norah suggested.

"Are you crazy? Of course I'm going to pay."

"That's no guarantee you'll get your son back."

The woman blanched, then her dark eyes blazed. "Yes, you've already made that clear. But if I don't pay, then I certainly won't ever see my child again."

"That's not necessarily true, Mrs. Millard," Norah said. It was the old controversy between police and parents that came up in every kidnapping, but to the parents it was fresh and new and painful.

"I have to pay," Adele Millard reiterated. "I'll raise the money somehow."

She was lucky that she could find a way to pay, Norah thought. In her own situation, when the life of their adopted son Mark had been threatened, there had been no way. Joe had wanted to call in the FBI and she had refused. She had done then what she thought best; could she now deny the same right to this woman? Norah took a deep breath.

"All right. Raise as much cash as you can. When he calls, offer it. He may be willing to accept and give you more time to raise the rest. I doubt very much he's going to turn you down completely."

Adele Millard bowed her head. Yolanda Yates went over and once again drew her into her arms. In the ensuing pause, the doorbell rang. The companion disengaged herself to go and answer. She brought back with her a tall, blond, bearded man.

"Addie," he said and went directly to his ex-wife. They stood close for several minutes silently consoling each other. Then the man broke away.

"Lieutenant Mulcahaney? I'm Richard Millard." He held out his hand. "Anything new?"

"The kidnapper has made his demand. He wants five hundred thousand by three this afternoon."

Millard formed a silent whistle. "Wilma will pay, won't she?" he asked his ex-wife.

"Mother's dead. She died trying to protect Todd."

Millard gasped. "Oh, Addie, I'm sorry. I'm so sorry. What can we do? How about asking Pete Bouchard? Why don't you sell him the Bonnard? He's always wanted it. At five hundred thou', it's a bargain. No, it's a steal."

"I don't have the right to sell it."

"Don't be stupid. Of course you do. It's all yours now—everything, all of it." He made an all-encompassing gesture. "Pete's not going to worry about formalities. Call him."

Still, Adele Millard hesitated and looked to Norah.

"You might feel better with the FBI to advise you."

"No!" Both parents responded at once.

"How many times do I have to tell you?" the mother added.

"I can't promise to get your money back," Norah told her.

"Forget the money. We don't care about the money. We care about our son. We don't care whether the kidnapper gets away." Millard's lips curled. "We just want Todd. Don't you understand?"

"I do and I sympathize, but this man, the kidnapper, is also a murderer. He's responsible for Wilma Danay's death," she reminded them both.

"Nothing can hurt my mother anymore," Adele Millard answered. "She's beyond pain, and vengeance can wait."

There was so much to do and very little time in which to do it. Peter Bouchard agreed to buy the Bonnard painting. As executor of the Danay estate, he accepted without question Adele's right to sell it. But of the five hundred thousand he was only able to make available two hundred thousand in cash by the deadline. There were added difficulties in that it was Veterans Day and most of the banks were closed. However, Bouchard promised to get the cash to her by the deadline.

Officially, Simon Wyler was carrying the case. With Ferdi

Arenas, Danny Neel, and Norah herself that made four who were present and aware of the situation. She had full confidence in these men. They were smart, dedicated, and, above all, resourceful. They could adjust to a changing situation. Nevertheless, she would have liked a few extras, just in case. The Millards, however, resisted when she suggested bringing in more people. They threatened to banish everyone including Norah and handle the entire transaction themselves.

Unexpectedly, Yolanda Yates came down on the side of the police.

"Addie, you can't handle this alone. For God's sake, darling, these people are experts. You've got to let them do what they think is right."

"Stay out of this, Yolanda," Millard snapped. "It's none of your business. This is a family matter."

"That's right and I'm part of this family; you're not," she retorted. "Not anymore. You walked out on Addie and Todd. Now you've got another wife and another child on the way. Addie has nobody but me."

"Todd is still my son!"

"You'd never know it from the interest you take."

"You don't know anything about the interest . . ."

"Stop it, stop it, both of you. Please!" Adele Millard cried out, her control breaking at last.

"You've upset her. See that? Aren't things difficult enough without your interfering?" Millard charged.

Yolanda Yates turned her back on him. "Why don't you let me handle this for you, baby?" she pleaded. "When the call comes, I'll take it . . ."

"What? Are you crazy?" Millard's face flamed. You'll ruin everything. I'll talk to him. I'm the father . . ."

It was time for Norah to restore order. "That's enough! Please. You can't afford to argue. You can't allow yourselves to be distracted or emotional. We must all be calm and completely focused when the next call comes. There's no question that anybody but Mrs. Millard must deal with it. Miss Yates, it might be best if you left us."

"No. I'm not leaving Addie. No way. I'm staying right here."

"Miss Yates . . ."

"Is that what you want, Addie? Do you want me to go?"

"Just for now. Please."

"If that's what you want." She nodded. "I'll be in my room." Casting a look of resentment at Richard Millard, she stalked out.

At five minutes of three, the messenger from the bank arrived as promised. Adele Millard signed the receipt for the cash and the messenger left. All eyes fixed on the mantelpiece clock. As the hands reached the hour, the chimes sounded three times. All eyes shifted to the telephone on the desk.

Nothing.

The desk phone was the regular one, the one on which the kidnapper had called earlier and would again. An extension with recording device had been added. There was also a second and separate line installed at Norah's order. It was on the long library table and was being monitored from her office at the station house. It would be used to activate a trace on the first line.

Five minutes passed, then ten.

Nobody said anything. Adele Millard squirmed in her chair; Professor Millard lit his pipe but let it quickly go out. The detectives remained quiet; if anything, they were more relaxed. On the surface.

Three-fifteen.

Adele Millard broke the silence. "He's not going to call, is he?"

"He's not that late, Mrs. Millard," Norah soothed. "He

could be delayed for any number of reasons. Maybe he intends to use a public telephone and it's occupied. Or he's playing on your nerves so that when he finally does make contact you'll be more willing to do what he wants. It's one of the ploys kidnappers use."

The detectives shifted in their seats and were still again. Professor Millard cleaned out his pipe. Adele Millard clasped her hands in her lap to keep them from trembling.

At three-thirty, the clock on the mantel chimed once and was immediately followed by the ring of the telephone.

Everybody looked to Adele Millard, who appeared paralyzed.

"Go ahead," Norah urged, standing ready beside the extension while Ferdi Arenas was alerting the station house. "Go on."

Adele Millard picked up and so did Norah. "Hello?"

"Have you got the money?"

"Yes. That is, I've got two hundred thousand in unmarked . . ."

"I told you five." The kidnapper's voice was low, guttural but not uncouth.

"I know. It's the best I could do. You didn't give me enough time. Most banks are closed today. By tomorrow, Tuesday, I'll have the rest of it. I promise."

"I can't wait till tomorrow."

It was more frustration than threat and as such the first sign of insecurity, Norah thought. She pointed a finger at Adele Millard, cueing her to a certain one of the variation of responses they had rehearsed.

"I want to talk to Todd. I have to know that he's all right."

"Shut up and listen."

It seemed to Norah that the caller was assuming a toughness not natural to him. Certainly, his control had wavered, if only for a brief moment.

"I'm going to hang up now, but I'll call back in one hour exactly and I want to talk to the old lady."

"You can't! I told you. She's had a heart attack." After a short pause, as rehearsed but full of real feeling, Adele Millard blurted, "My God, she's dead!"

There was a deep silence.

"One hour," he said and hung up.

Norah put down the extension, then went over to Adele Millard and had to take the receiver out of her hand and hang up for her. "We've rattled him. He needs time to think."

"Will he call back?"

"Oh yes, we can count on that," Norah replied. "You did well, Mrs. Millard." She would have liked to offer more reassurance but she didn't want the woman to relax too much. "So, while he's making his decision we have to make ours. We have to decide . . ."

"There's nothing for us to decide," Richard Millard snapped. "We're going to do what he tells us."

"That's understood," Norah replied and was silent to let the atmosphere cool. Danny Neel went into the kitchen to make coffee, and everyone welcomed the short respite. Once again Norah reviewed with the Millards the options at the kidnapper's disposal and how they might deal with whichever he chose. There would be no games; he would get right down to business. If he decided to take the two hundred thousand, he would give instructions for the delivery. These would have to be followed precisely. At the same time, they would have to be prepared to tail him after the money was turned over.

"No!" Adele Millard cried out.

"We told you before, we don't give a damn about the money," Millard backed her.

"It's not for the money," Norah sighed. "How do we know he intends to return your son?"

The parents looked at each other in dismay. "Why shouldn't he?"

"Maybe because your son can identify him."

The mother turned white; the father groaned.

"If you follow him or whoever picks up the ransom, how do you know he'll lead you back to Todd?" Millard demanded.

"We don't." That was as much as Norah intended to say. If the kidnapper agreed to take the two hundred thousand, it could very well mean he wasn't able to deliver the child because Todd was already dead. That possibility hadn't occurred to the Millards, Norah thought, but every officer in the room was certainly aware of it. The first indication that the kidnapper would accept what had been offered was the ringing of the telephone at precisely sixty minutes after the first call as promised, or threatened.

As before, Adele Millard, Norah, and Ferdi synchronized their action.

"Hello?"

"Shut up and listen. As soon as I hang up, you get a shopping bag and put the case with the money into it. You've got two minutes to do that. You've got two more minutes to take the elevator down to the lobby and walk out the front door. I'll be watching. If you're late by so much as ten seconds, the deal is off. Understand?"

"Yes, I understand. I'll have the money in a shopping bag and be out of the building in four minutes."

"Start walking up Second Avenue. Stay near the building line and hold the shopping bag in your left hand. Got that?"

"Yes."

"Keep walking. Be sure you're alone and nobody is following you. If anyone tries to apprehend the person who approaches you or follows him, you'll never see your son again. Got that?"

"Yes, I'll do everything as you say. I promise. When do I get Todd back?"

"One hour after the money is delivered you'll be told where to find him."

"No, that's not good enough!" Desperation made her strong. "I want you to give me my son when I give you the money. He has to be there or . . ." she stopped. "Hello? Hello?" Dazed, helpless, she announced, "He hung up."

Norah checked her watch: four-thirty-one with the second hand sweeping inexorably to four-thirty-two. "Where are the old shopping bags?"

Adele Millard was breathing heavily. "In the kitchen, somewhere," she gasped.

"Get one," Norah told Neel and she didn't need to add—fast.

By the time he returned with a Bloomie's Big Brown Bag, her watch indicated fifty more seconds had passed. She put the money case into the bag and handed it to Mrs. Millard.

"You do exactly what he told you and don't worry about anything else, okay?"

"I don't know. I wish . . . Wouldn't it be better if you didn't try to follow me? I really think . . ."

"You're wasting time, Mrs. Millard. Please. You've got to get going. Now." Norah just about pushed her to the door and out into the corridor to the elevator.

They had been holding one of the two passenger elevators on the floor along with the service car so there was no waiting. As soon as the doors closed on Mrs. Millard clutching the shopping bag in her left hand as ordered, Norah and Wyler and Neel got on the service elevator. At the basement exit, Norah reminded them, "You keep about half a block ahead on the other side of the street. I'll stay on this side about half a block behind."

Wyler and Neel walked out first, crossed Second Avenue, and started what appeared to be a leisurely stroll uptown.

After a short wait, Norah emerged. Immediately, she looked ahead to locate Mrs. Millard. She should have had no trouble getting out of the building and on the street in the four minutes allotted, but when she didn't see her right away, Norah's heart began to race and she grew hot with anxiety. She forced herself to stay calm and behave casually while searching the crowd. Mrs. Millard was wearing the same navy outfit she'd arrived in. It was anything but conspicuous and that might serve to allay the perp's suspicions about a tail. His plan was simple but effective, Norah thought grudgingly, made more so by the fact that she and the two detectives were walking uptown while the traffic was one way downtown. In other words, they were working against the traffic and couldn't use a car as part of the tail. A simple part of the plan, but effective. At that moment, Norah spotted the subject. No wonder she hadn't seen her right away; Adele Millard was much farther ahead than expected. She was moving too fast. At least, she still had the shopping bag. Norah quickened her pace.

The subject reached Seventy-second Street where she was forced to stop at the curb and wait for the light. Relieved, Norah was able to close the distance between them. When Millard started across the wide intersection, Norah was half a block behind as originally intended. On the other side of the avenue, the men adjusted their pace.

The light held up the subject again on Seventy-ninth and then on Eighty-sixth. Norah kept adjusting her pace. How long was this going to keep up? Did he intend to collect the money or was this merely a rehearsal? Had he made them? Norah was beginning to have doubts. How long would Adele Millard last? How long could she? By now she must be very upset and uncertain, not to say tired. The kidnapper had instructed that she should carry the shopping bag in her left hand and keep close to the building line, suggesting that someone would emerge from a store or lobby, grab the bag, and disappear into the crowd. So as she walked, Norah scanned the doorways just ahead for loiterers. Her attention was on those doorways except when the subject was at the curb waiting to cross.

It happened at Ninety-sixth. The light was yellow and about to turn red. A pedestrian, male Caucasian, in jeans and matching jacket, crossed the street from the opposite side. As he passed Adele Millard, he said something to her— naturally Norah had no idea what. He took the bag. As he did so, a white compact going crosstown pulled up. The passenger door opened and he got in. The door slammed shut. The car shot across the intersection narrowly escaping collision with the phalanx of traffic headed downtown.

Nothing they could do but watch.

Except when performed by terrorists, kidnapping was usually a once in a lifetime crime performed by amateurs, Norah thought. This kidnapping had been particularly inept. The perpetrator had made so much noise breaking in that Wilma Danay had been alerted and he'd had to use brute force to subdue her. As a result of that, the boy had barricaded himself and the perp' had to force the door. Picking a Sunday night when the following Monday was a legal holiday was another serious error, Norah thought. On the other hand, he had shown himself resourceful regarding the pickup. He was in possession of the money. Would he keep his word and turn over the child?

Norah watched Adele Millard. She stood at the curb, rigid. A group of pedestrians had formed around her. They were talking to her and she was shaking her head. Probably they were asking if she needed help, if she wanted the police, and she was saying no. Norah kept her distance as a precaution; she was sure there was nobody around to check. Meanwhile, Adele disengaged herself from her would-be helpers, and hailed a cab.

Norah headed for Lexington Avenue and the subway. Wyler and Neel trailed behind.

They all got on the Number Six train and got off at Lexington and Fifty-ninth. They walked down to the lower level toward the far end of the platform. An escalator brought them up to Third Avenue and Sixtieth.

Twenty minutes later, at five-fifty-one P.M., a woman fell or was pushed to the tracks from that very platform. Power was shut off along the line from Fifty-ninth to a Hundred and Twenty-fifth Streets.

By then, Norah, Wyler, and Neel were back in the Danay apartment.

Adele Millard had left the building with the money at precisely four-thirty-five. After forty minutes of walking, the bag had been taken from her at five-fifteen. Therefore, the call revealing Todd's whereabouts was due at six-fifteen, an hour later.

Again, they waited: Adele Millard, Norah, the two detectives who had been on the tail, and Ferdi Arenas, who had stayed behind with Richard Millard. There was no coffee this time, no attempt at conversation. The hands of the clock reached six. The chimes pealed. The hands moved on to the quarter hour.

"Why doesn't he call?" Adele Millard didn't direct the question to anyone in particular.

"He could have meant an hour after you got back," her ex-husband suggested. "What do you think, Lieutenant?"

"It's possible." Norah's own hopes were fading fast.

As the single chime marked the half hour at six-thirty, Adele Millard could no longer contain herself. She jumped to her feet. "He's not going to call. He's not going to give Todd back, is he?" This question was directed at Norah.

"I don't know," she replied.

"It's your fault. He warned me not to let anyone follow me."

"I don't believe he was aware of the surveillance."

"You don't believe? Of course he was! Of course. He warned me and I didn't listen. I let you talk me into doing it your way. I had confidence in you. I thought, as a woman, you understood my feelings. I trusted you. I was wrong. All you care about is making an arrest. You don't care about my child."

The rebuke hurt, but Norah didn't respond. She felt Ferdi's eyes on her and shook her head almost imperceptibly to indicate she didn't want anything about Mark said.

"Addie. Addie, darling," Richard Millard embraced his ex-wife. "He might still call. Don't give up. After all, he didn't get the full amount he wanted; so very probably he will call and try to get the rest. He could be putting us through this to soften us up. Isn't that right, Lieutenant?"

"It's very possible," Norah agreed. "It may be a long wait, though. I'll stay with you, of course."

"No!" the distraught woman snapped. "I don't want you here. I don't want anybody, not you, not your detectives, not the FBI. If he calls, I'll answer and I'll deal with him. It would be better if I'd never listened to you. Go away. Everybody go away."

"There's a lot we can do, Mrs. Millard," Norah pleaded. "We've far from exhausted the possibilities; actually, we haven't even begun. We can make up flyers with Todd's picture and description. We'll flood the neighborhood and the airports and the rail terminals. More than ninety percent of missing children are recovered."

The woman glared at Norah. "Really? Did you see who was driving the car? Did you get the license number? Did anybody? Did you or your detectives even get the license number?"

"No," Norah admitted. There had been too many obstacles—cars and pedestrians—in the way. Besides, the car was probably stolen or carrying false plates, so the number would have been useless. But Norah forebore to point out any of this. "I'm sorry" was all she said.

"You should be."

And now, Norah thought, the FBI wouldn't even want the case. It had been botched, they would claim.

They would be right.

Chapter

EIGHT

Joanna Christie worked nights as a cocktail waitress down in the Village. She got through at midnight but seldom went straight home uptown. She usually had a late date, or if not, went with a girlfriend to one of the discos. She was a pretty woman with a mane of dark hair that she liked to toss so that it swirled around her pale face, its palor accentuated by bright red lips and dark eyes outlined in khol. The current style of short, tight skirts permitted her to show off firm buttocks and long, lean legs. She had taken the waitressing job and stuck to it with the idea of meeting men. She did meet them and got plenty of dates, but they weren't leading anywhere. Joanna Christie was thirty-two and beginning to have nagging doubts about her future. She noticed that the late nights were leaving their mark; her face and body were both beginning to sag. To counteract, she'd started to take a short nap in the afternoon just before going to work.

Unfortunately, on Monday, November twelfth, Joanna Christie forgot to set her alarm and her mental monitor didn't rouse her till five o'clock. That triggered a series of minor misshaps that further delayed her. Usually she had a couple of cups of coffee to wake up, but today she measured out the water and the coffee and then neglected to plug in the electric pot. Dressing in a hurry, she broke a fingernail and snagged her panty hose. More time was lost taking them off and putting on a new pair. Once one thing went wrong, Joanna thought with exasperation as she watched her train pull into the station while she was still at the top of the escalator, everything went wrong. No use running; she wouldn't make it. But the doors stayed open longer than she expected. Just as she decided to try for it after all, they closed.

One good thing about being late and trying to make up the time, Joanna mused, was that she'd forgotten about *him*. The walk from her building to the subway entrance on Third Avenue and Sixtieth was only four short blocks. Lately, since the coming of fall, she'd noticed more homeless people in the neighborhood. There was one in particular, in the same place every afternoon, whom she came to recognize and after a while to look for. She wasn't sure when she'd first become aware of him or why. Naturally, she'd ignored him. Didn't all New Yorkers ignore the homeless? Hadn't we all learned not to look too closely? Joanna Christie knew that these unfortunates staked out "space" like mendicants of old, so she wasn't surprised to see him regularly, leaning against the corner of the bank on Sixty-fourth Street, a cigarette dangling from his mouth. He was younger than most of the homeless, or were they all getting younger, the men and the women? He was tall, that is he would be if he stood straight, and she had a hunch that under the rags he was well built. Once she'd met his blue-gray eyes directly, but she'd quickly looked away. It wasn't good to look at these people straight on. They could take offense, turn nasty. Victims of society, they were not all quiescent. Like most ordinary citizens, Joanna Christie both pitied and feared them.

This man, this tall, almost good-looking, sad man in his rags, a cord tied around his waist, bare feet in flapping sandals, intrigued her. She observed him several days in a row before he started to follow her. He kept a distance, and Joanna told herself he just happened to be going her way. As long as he didn't go down into the subway after her, she could believe that's all it was. Then a week ago precisely, a Monday, she had reached the platform and happened to look back up and there he was at the top of the escalator on the way down. Her train came and she got on while he was still a distance away.

The next couple of times, though he followed more closely and was able to reach the platform while she was still waiting, he hadn't approached. In fact, once he'd gotten on a train on the other side that was heading uptown, while she waited to go downtown. Wasn't that proof he wasn't following her?

Today, she'd been too preoccupied to look for him. She was just congratulating herself for getting rid of the phobia when she saw him. He was at the far end and coming toward her. He was making his way through the crowd with purpose, she thought as she watched, mesmerized. He wouldn't do anything to her here. Not with all these people around. Ignore him, she told herself. Don't look at him. Don't let him know you're afraid. Why should she be afraid? Joanna asked herself. The man was a stranger.

I don't know him, she thought. *I've never done anything to him. Why should he want to harm me?*

There was panic on the platform. People around him were running, pushing, shoving to get out. Nathaniel Gorin let himself be carried by the tide to the escalator and back up to the street.

He emerged into an area of motion picture theaters, stores, and fast-food restaurants. Suddenly, he was ravenously hungry. There was a McDonald's on the block. He went in, had a quarter pounder with everything on it. When he came out, dusk was melting into night. He hesitated, then decided to follow the usual pattern. He noticed that a long line formed in front of one of the theaters was just starting to move.

He walked up to the ticket booth and shoved the exact change at the teller. She gawked. Nobody like that, ragged and dirty, obviously one of the homeless, had ever come up to her window. How many of the homeless had that kind of money? And could spend it on a movie? What should she do? His eyes glittered malevolently as he looked into hers. What could she do? She issued the ticket and Nathaniel Gorin went inside.

He found a seat at the back. The picture, whatever it was, was scheduled to run two hours. Just before it was over, Gorin left his seat and went into the men's room.

Making sure he was alone, he took off the threadbare blanket with a hole for his head that served as a tunic, then his baggy, stained pants. He pulled off the knitted merchant seaman's cap and rolled everything into a tight ball, stuffing it into a plastic bag that he took from a deep pocket. These formed the outer layer. Underneath he had on brown slacks and a tweed jacket over a turtle-necked pullover, all creased but clean and unremarkable. He washed his face and combed his hair. *Not bad,* he thought, looking at himself in the mirror.

The sound track coming in over the loudspeakers told him precisely when the film was over. He emerged from the lavatory to join the crowd on the way out.

He was home and in bed by nine P.M. and fell instantly into a heavy sleep. He slept untroubled by dreams.

Told to leave, Norah Mulcahaney and her team had no choice but to comply with Adele Millard's wish. They returned to the station house to wait. By midnight it was clear to all that the kidnapper would not be calling, at least not anytime soon.

A scant twenty-four hours had passed since the murder and kidnapping, so the trail was still fresh. It was decided that no purpose would be served by continuing to keep Wilma Danay's death a secret, and so the events of the night of November eleventh were released to the media.

"Okay," Norah said, addressing the three detectives. "The top priority remains the boy."

"You think he's alive?" Wyler asked bluntly.

"We don't know he isn't," she retorted. "From now on, everything we do, every move we make, is going to be predicated on the assumption that Todd Millard *is* alive." She took a deep breath and leaned back in her chair. Just having said it made her feel better.

"We need to know, first of all, how the perp' got him out of the building. Obviously, he didn't take him out the front; they would have been seen. So they went out the back. Certainly, the boy didn't go willingly—unless he was rendered unconscious, in which case he would have had to be carried . . . to a car maybe. There's a lot of action in that area on Second and Third Avenues: movie theaters, restaurants, all kinds of stores. They stay open late, which means people are milling around. Someone may have noticed something.

"So, Ferdi, I want a canvass mounted now, tonight, to cover a four-block square area around that building. Ask Sergeant Brennan if he can spare any uniforms to help us. You work with Ferdi," she told Danny Neel.

"A photo would help," he said.

"Well, we haven't got one and Mrs. Millard isn't disposed to provide one. But the boy was in his pajamas. That should make him memorable."

"Right."

"Simon, I'm interested in Wilma Danay's will," she told

Wyler. "Find out who drew it up and make an appointment for me to see him as soon as possible. I'm going to grab some sleep."

They knew she wasn't going home, but would be using one of the cots in the women's lounge. Later, after their assignments, Wyler and the others would get some rest right there in the station house as well. It would be a while before any of the squad slept in their own beds.

Nathaniel Gorin woke at his usual time on Tuesday morning. He felt well rested. The day was gloomy but it didn't affect him. Rain was predicted; he didn't care. As he got ready to go to work—he was manager of one of a chain of electronics stores in midtown—bits and pieces of the events of the past night came back to him, out of order, disconnected. He turned on the radio. There was no mention of what had happened underground. The newscaster and the commentators were talking of only one thing—the murder of Wilma Danay and the disappearance of her grandson. When he got to the store, the salesmen were standing around talking of nothing else. It got on his nerves, and at eleven he slammed out, saying he was going for an early lunch.

"What's bugging him?" The younger man who had been hired only a couple of months back wanted to know.

The older, who had been there a couple of years, shrugged. "He gets like that every so often. It passes."

But Nathaniel Gorin hadn't left because he was hungry. He wanted to see the newspapers, so he headed for the newstand on Forty-fifth.

The temperature had dropped and the wind was sharp, but Gorin didn't notice. He bought the three local tabloids and the *Times* and then went to his favorite luncheonette, which at this hour was just about empty. He settled himself in a rear booth. As on previous occasions, the story he was looking for was buried on an inside page. The reporter showed more concern for the disruption of service and the inconvenience to the passengers than for the woman who had been run over. Gorin felt his blood heat up. Little was said about the victim. A woman had died, but they didn't care. They knew it was more than an accident. They knew all right, but they didn't want to admit it because then they'd have to do something and they were lazy. Lazy and incompetent.

The piece in the *Post* ended with a couple of terse lines:

A month ago a similar incident in which a woman fell to the tracks and was killed occurred at the same station.

It was almost an afterthought.

Tuesday nights the store stayed open till nine. Gorin locked up and then took the bus home. It had begun to rain. He'd missed the early newscasts, so he decided to catch the ten o'clock edition at Finn's. He showered, changed to gray slacks and a navy blazer. By the time he was ready, the rain was coming down hard, so he decided to wear a raincoat and take an umbrella.

When he walked in, the neighborhood hangout was full. The regulars were lined up two and three deep at the bar and the stool he usually occupied was taken. He said nothing, merely stood at the edge of the crowd, but they made room for him. As he fixed his mild eyes on the occupant of his stool, the man got off.

"Working late again, Nat?" The bartender's question was more in the nature of a comment as he set out Gorin's usual draft beer. Above the heads of the customers the television was tuned in to the news. A reporter was interviewing neighbors of Wilma Danay. They were eulogizing her.

"I'm sick and tired of hearing about that woman," Nat Gorin complained. "So she had a heart attack. Who cares? She's not the only one. Put on the football game."

"There's no football tonight."

"Hockey then."

"No hockey either."

"Then turn the damn thing off."

Chapter

NINE

Norah woke at six-thirty Tuesday morning, more or less her usual time. But her sleep had been fitful and she still felt groggy. She sent out for breakfast and while waiting went to the women's lounge for a quick shower. Back in her office, she found a note from Simon Wyler on her desk.

Wilma Danay's legal affairs were handled by Jerome Ritter, 250 Madison Avenue. He's in Europe on business and won't be back for another ten days.

She ate breakfast to the accompaniment of the noisy bustle of the changing watch. At eight precisely, she dialed the Danay number. Adele Millard answered promptly.

"This is Lieutenant Mulcahaney, Mrs. Millard." Norah hesitated only for a moment. "Any news?"

"Nothing." Todd's mother sounded tired and discouraged.

"I think we should put out the flyers, Mrs. Millard."

"Please get off the phone, Lieutenant. You're tying up the line." Adele Millard hung up first.

Poor woman, Norah thought. She stepped out into the squad room. Neither Arenas nor Neel had returned. Wyler, of course, was there. He went over as soon as he saw her.

"Jerome Ritter is in London till the end of the week. Then he goes on to Paris. If you want to reach him now, he's at the Park Lane."

"We'll see. I want to talk to the Bouchards first and I want you to visit Nick Kouriades. Find out what his financial situation is. Ask him if he has any idea who might have snatched the boy."

"You think it's an inside job? If it is and the boy recognized him . . ." He shook his head.

"You're jumping to conclusions. I will not accept that Todd Millard is dead until I have to. I thought I made that clear."

"Yes, ma'am."

She eased up. "I'll be at the Bouchards if anybody wants me."

The Bouchards lived on Central Park West, a short, brisk walk from the station house. After several days of unseasonably warm weather, a cold front sweeping in during the night had brought a sharp tang to the air. Norah was wearing the gray slacks and sweater Kathryn Webber had brought over to her at the Danay apartment, but the wind went right through her. She quickened her pace and by the time she reached the Bouchards' building she was well awake and tingling with energy. It was nine-twenty-one A.M., the middle of the night for theatrical people.

Norah had no compunction about rousing the couple and she had no doubt they would agree to see her despite the early hour. They were the only ones outside the immediate family and Yolanda Yates and the staff of Wilma Danay's building, who had known about the kidnapping before the story was released. Bouchard had, after all, provided the ransom money, so he would be expecting a visit from the police. She was not surprised that when she gave her name to the doorman and he announced her on the house phone, he was told to send her right up.

A small man, partially bald, dressed in a way that immediately identified him as a houseman—black pants, white shirt, striped vest and black bow tie—was waiting for Norah. He ushered her into a spacious room flooded with a cool north light and left her. She looked around with great interest. The decor was modern. There was a large, curving sectional in black leather and a heavy free-form crystal cocktail table; bare floors, highly polished; no clutter of knickknacks. The lighting was designed to show off the paintings on the walls. The whole was a marked contrast to Wilma Danay's fragile, period-style apartment, yet each served as background for a breathtaking array of art.

Off to one side, but not to be ignored, was a black-lacquered vitrine in which were displayed the photographs, mementoes, and trophies of Peter Bouchard's career. Norah walked over to examine them. There were studio shots of the actor, alone and with his great so-star, Wilma Danay. Some included Quentin Noble. There were snapshots, fading reminders of parties held in sumptuous mansions, beside pools, on the decks of yachts.

"Good morning." The actor's sonorous voice boomed out like a Shakespearean fanfare.

The Bouchards, Peter and Camilla, made their entrance together. He was as massive as a Buddha, barely recognizable under the layers of flesh as the handsome leading man in the pictures she had just now been scrutinizing, Norah thought. He was wearing an elaborate, heavy silk robe with a black satin shawl collar, and he moved slowly, laboriously, till he reached the nearest chair and sank into it. Norah now understood why the furniture was so massive.

"I apologize for disturbing you this early."

"In the old days a six A.M. call on the set wasn't unusual,

and that meant being in makeup and costume," Bouchard replied. "Anyway, we were awake."

Camilla Bouchard was petite. Next to her husband's enormous bulk she was almost childlike. "We've been awake for hours," she said.

She looked it, Norah thought. Her eyes were red and swollen. The shadows underneath the heavy makeup were easily discernible. Though her hair was short and straight and should have been easy to care for, it lacked lustre. Her thin fingers, tipped with bright red polish, played with the tasseled ends of the gold cord around the waist of her pink satin robe.

Bouchard waved Norah to the sofa. "Is there any news?"

"I assume you know that the money was paid but Todd has not been returned," she answered. "So far, there's been no further contact by the kidnapper. That is, not as of eight this morning when I spoke to Mrs. Millard."

"What's being done?"

"The situation is difficult. Mrs. Millard feels that the presence of the police or FBI would deter the kidnapper from seeking further communication. She wants to handle everything herself."

"Under the circumstances . . ." Bouchard sighed heavily.

"As I understand it, neither Professor nor Mrs. Millard, that is the first Mrs. Millard, have a lot of money. It appears that the kidnapping was done with an eye to making Miss Danay pay for the child's return. I understand she was devoted to the boy."

"All wrapped up in him. Thought the world of him." Bouchard smiled sadly. "She would have paid any price to get him back."

"Did Todd stay with her on a regular basis?" Norah had asked that question before and would ask it again of various witnesses.

"Not regularly, but frequently, and on those occasions Wilma canceled all other plans and devoted herself exclusively to him. In fact, since yesterday was a school holiday, Wilma had planned to take him to see that Ninja Turtles movie." He shook his head, marveling at the extent of her devotion. "She would have been happy to have the boy with her on a permanent basis, but she felt it wouldn't be good for him. She thought a child should be with his parents; at least one of them. That's why she didn't do the room over for him. She wanted him to regard home as where his mother lived."

"I see."

"Wilma disapproved of Adele's life-style, but what could she say? Adele parried her mother's criticism by pointing out that Wilma herself had married three times and had who knows how many affairs in between. Wilma had shunted Adele from one private boarding school to another. Todd at least was at home with one or the other parent or with his beloved 'Nana.' "

"They didn't get along then, mother and daughter?"

Bouchard shook his head. "And yet they were more alike than either realized or cared to admit. Adele was always in her mother's shadow. She tried hard to match her success, but she didn't have the talent. She just didn't have it. When Wilma and I were married, I tried to instill some self-confidence in the girl, but she didn't want my help. So, since she couldn't match her mother's theatrical success, she tried to match her sexual exploits. Wilma's first marriage was at sixteen. At eighteen, Adele had an affair with Richard and got pregnant. Wilma insisted they get married. Richard was amenable. I believe he loved Adele, and becoming Wilma Danay's son-in-law was an agreeable prospect.

"After a while, it became evident that being the wife of a professor didn't suit Adele. Being a mother didn't, either.

Finally, after a series of failures as an actress, she found a career in advertising. We all thought that settled it. But we didn't factor in Richard. He wanted his wife waiting for him at home with dinner on the table. He wanted her to be a gracious hostess, to serve on committees, and remain in the background. I believe the divorce was as mutually agreeable as it could be. There was no community property to squabble over, only the child. They both wanted Todd. It was ugly for a while."

"But now that Professor Millard has remarried and is expecting another child by his second wife, doesn't he feel differently?" Norah wanted to know.

"According to Wilma—no. Millard's position is that Todd is still his son and he is willing and able to offer the boy a stable home and permanent family. Which his ex-wife can't or doesn't want to do."

Norah looked hard at the actor. "Are you suggesting parental kidnapping?"

"I think you should consider it, Lieutenant. He did know that the boy would be with Wilma over the weekend."

"A great many people knew that," Norah pointed out. "His teachers, schoolmates, the staff of the building where he lived with his mother, and the staff of Miss Danay's building. You and your wife knew. So did Mr. Kouriades."

Bouchard shrugged. "It was just a thought."

"Parental kidnapping usually involves one of the parents snatching the child from the other and absconding with him to another state where the court that awarded custody to the mate has no jurisdiction. Such is not the case here. Professor Millard has not run away. His second wife is about to give birth, and there is no indication he intends to move away afterwards."

"I thought I should mention it." Bouchard cast a look at his wife.

She cleared her throat. "May we offer you coffee, Lieutenant?"

"No, thank you. Unless . . . are you having some?"

"Well, we haven't had breakfast yet so, yes, we will."

"In that case, I'll join you. Thank you."

Rising gracefully, Camilla Bouchard went over to the antique bell pull and gave it a tug. The houseman appeared promptly.

"We'll all have coffee, please, William."

Camilla was younger than Norah had thought, a lot younger than either her husband or Wilma Danay. "How long have you and Mr. Bouchard been married?" Norah asked.

"Twelve years this coming month," she announced with pride.

"Congratulations."

"Most of our friends didn't think we'd last a year."

"How did you meet?"

"Peter and Wilma were doing a road tour of *Private Lives.* I read for the second woman and they hired me."

"Wilma and I were no longer married at that time," Bouchard volunteered.

"I see."

"I'm not sure you do, Lieutenant," he chided. "Wilma and I were friends, good friends. We were friends before the marriage and friends after. Not during." His eyes twinkled, and it was evident this was a little joke he repeated frequently.

The houseman brought the coffee in a silver pot on a silver tray and poured into bone china cups. They were silent during the ceremony. When he left, Norah resumed.

"What can you tell me about Yolanda Yates?" She didn't direct the question specifically to one or the other, and it was Peter Bouchard who chose to answer.

"Yolanda was hired initially to answer the fan mail. She

was young and she idolized Wilma. In no time at all, she became Wilma's personal secretary, paid her bills, took care of her appointments, and so on. During our marriage, Yolanda ran the house and the staff. After our divorce, Wilma invited her to move in, and she became a combination secretary-housekeeper-companion."

"How about Nick Kouriades?"

"A true theatrical talent," Bouchard pronounced. "He started as an apprentice to one of our great set designers, Jo Mielziner, worked himself up to running his own shop, and now he's a producer. Wilma invested in several of his shows. So did I, and we both made money."

"Several, but not all?"

"Of course not all. Wilma was a very shrewd investor, Lieutenant. She learned a lot from her first husband, Frank Grillo, Adele's father. She didn't trust her money to just anybody or any project. When it came to money, friendship was not a consideration."

He hadn't said an unkind word about anybody, Norah thought. Even when he'd implied that Richard Millard might be guilty of kidnapping his own son, he'd done it without rancor. It was an effective technique.

"So there were occasions when Kouriades went to Miss Danay for money and was turned down?"

"He has a script now that he's very hot on, but Wilma didn't share his enthusiasm."

"Was he able to get the money somewhere else?"

"Probably. Whether he was or not, I wouldn't attach too much significance to it. A lot of people went to Wilma for money and she turned them down. You have to realize, Lieutenant, that a star like Wilma Danay is surrounded by sycophants, people who want something from her, people who have neither the talent nor the ability nor the will to work and achieve on their own merits."

"Would you give me some names?"

Bouchard shook his head. "I don't know them all. It wouldn't be fair." With a Buddhalike serenity, the actor folded his hands across his stomach, marking the end of the subject.

"You did a lot of business with Miss Danay. You went into a lot of deals outside of show business together."

Either he didn't catch the implication or it didn't disturb him. "That's right. Some actors throw their money away as though it was coming from an inexhaustible source and they end up in the Actors' Home. Early on, Wilma and I swore it wouldn't happen to us." With a sweep of his hand he indicated the paintings that glowed on his walls. "Beautiful and lucrative. Wilma and I went to auctions together. We studied the artist and the market and then we bid. Never in competition. Sometimes supporting each other in the acquisition."

"And those acquisitions appreciated in value."

"That was the idea." He pointed. "The Kandinsky: I paid seventy-five thousand; it's worth two and a half million today. One example."

"So Miss Danay has left a very large estate."

"Indeed. In addition to the art collection, there are stocks, bonds, the apartment. Oh yes, very large," Bouchard agreed.

Simon Wyler rang the bell of the loft on East Twentieth at least four times before he got an answer and was buzzed in. He took the manually operated freight elevator up to the top floor where Nicholas Kouriades in robe and slippers was waiting on the landing.

He was a small, dessicated-looking man. His black hair, though heavily streaked with gray, was still thick. His skin was the color of varnished mahogany, suggesting the regular use of a sun lamp. He affected a mustache that was hardly more than a pencil line. Simon pegged him at somewhere around seventy. His dark eyes were bloodshot.

"Detective Wyler, Homicide." Simon showed his open shield case.

The *homicide* designation had its effect: Kouriades fell back and Wyler moved in.

He could see that the structural improvements required by most lofts to make them livable—walls repaired and freshly plastered, new floor of natural oak laid, installation of kitchen and bath and, presumably, the plumbing and wiring to go with it—had been done. Then, apparently, the project had stalled. No valuable paintings hung on these walls; they were decorated with posters of the designer's theatrical and film productions. His current work was on a draughtman's table. Three-dimensional miniaturizations were displayed on a trestle table in front of the metal housing for the burner. Kouriades had either run out of money or lost interest in the project, Wyler thought. However, as loft styling tended toward stark simplicity, and since part of the space was used for workshop and office, it looked and was functional and therefore acceptable.

Kouriades cast one quick glance toward the single partition, which Wyler assumed hid the sleeping arrangements. He sensed movement behind it.

"What can I do for you, Detective?" Kouriades asked.

"Have you had your radio or television on this morning?"

"No."

"Or seen a paper?"

"No."

"Then you haven't heard about Wilma Danay's death?"

Kouriades simply gaped. "Death? Wilma's dead?"

"She had a heart attack."

There was a long silence. "I didn't know she had a heart condition."

"And the boy, Todd Millard, is missing. Kidnapped. Did you know that?"

"No! My God! When did all this happen?"

"Sunday night after you and the Bouchards left."

Kouriades groaned. He broke out into a cold sweat. Abruptly, he turned and headed for the kitchen area. He got a bottle out of one of the cabinets and an old-fashioned glass and poured himself a generous measure, which he knocked back.

"Wilma dead, just like that. I can't believe it." He shook his head.

"Not exactly 'just like that,' " Wyler told him.

"What do you mean?"

"I'd like to ask you a few questions about Sunday night."

"Sure. Anything. My God, I can't believe it," he repeated.

"You and Wilma Danay were old friends?"

"Absolutely. Yes. Old friends and good friends. I did the sets for her last picture, *Paris Spring.*" He gestured toward one of the posters in the main area. "It didn't do well, the movie that is." He sighed, bit his lip. "Let's be honest; it was a flop. Not Wilma's fault. Her part wasn't big enough. The public went to see her, and she didn't have enough to do and they were disappointed."

"The bridge game? That was a regular game every Sunday?"

"Unless somebody was sick or out of town."

"You always played at Miss Danay's?"

"No. We took turns hosting."

"Did you play for big stakes?"

For the first time Kouriades relaxed. "A tenth of a cent a point, Detective. It was for the sociability."

"Anyway, this Sunday was different from the others?"

Kouriades shook his head. "We quit a little early, around ten, that's all. Wilma had to get up the next morning to take the boy somewhere—a museum, the movies, I don't know. It was a school holiday."

"She was devoted to the child?"

"He was the most important thing in her life."

"And everybody knew it?"

"Sure."

Wyler nodded. "So, the game broke up earlier than usual. Had the boy already gone to bed?"

"Oh sure. Wilma was good to him, but she was strict."

"So after the game broke up, what did you do?"

"Me, personally?" Kouriades shrugged. "Nothing. I came home."

"What time?"

"I don't know. I took a taxi. There wasn't much traffic. I didn't notice when I got here. Why?"

Wyler stared at him. "Did you sleep well?"

"What?"

"After the game broke up and you all left, somebody gained entry to Miss Danay's apartment. We don't know exactly how. He attacked her. She resisted. There was a violent struggle. She was brutally beaten, knocked sense-less." Wyler paused. One of the techniques favored by Lieu-tenant Mulcahaney was to feed out details of a crime slowly, letting the witness anticipate what was coming next.

Kouriades obliged.

"The beating brought on the heart attack, is that it? And you're suggesting that I went back after the game? That I had something to do with Wilma's death and the boy's kidnapping?" Fire burned under his mahogany skin; his bleary eyes filled. "I loved Wilma. I don't mean in a roman-tic way; I mean as an artist. Damn it to hell, I loved and respected that woman! She was beautiful . . ." He tapped his chest. "Inside and out. They don't make them like that anymore."

Still Wyler waited.

"Wilma was my friend. She backed me in three different shows." He indicated another group of posters. "Just a few weeks ago I showed her a new script and she was enthusiastic. We were getting ready to go into production."

The lieut' had the right idea, Wyler thought; Kouriades had volunteered an answer to a question he, Wyler, hadn't even asked. But was he telling the truth?

"Do you have your financing?"

"I have what I need."

"That's good, because now that she's dead you won't be getting any money from her," Wyler pointed out. Once more he paused for a comment or reaction, but this time was disappointed. "Unless . . . Are you mentioned in Miss Danay's will?"

"I have no idea."

"Well," Wyler got up. "If you could only remember what time you got home. Even if you could remember what kind of cab you took when you left Miss Danay's? No? The doorman will probably remember, and we can check the driver's call sheet."

"That won't be necessary," Kouriades said. "I didn't come straight home Sunday night. I had the cab drop me at a local bar. I met a friend there. He came home with me." He made a point of keeping his eyes averted from the bedroom partition.

Why? Wyler wondered.

"How fortuitous," he said.

Chapter

TEN

It was midnight Monday when Norah ordered the search of
the immediate area around the Danay apartment building,
and by two-thirty A.M. on Tuesday, Sergeant Arenas had a
modest force out on the streets.

This city, a center for the arts and industry and the financial capital of the world, was becoming infamous as a strong-
hold of criminals. Like Norah, Ferdi Arenas was particularly
disturbed by what was happening to the children. They were
being randomly murdered on the streets, in cars parked in
their home driveways, and even in their own homes. A
society that cannot protect its young is marked for extinc-
tion, he thought. He felt a strong empathy for the parents of
Todd Millard and rage at the kidnapper. How could anyone
put a child through such an ordeal? There was so little to go
on, and though the canvass would cover a relatively small
section, it was a densely populated one and attracted a large
number of visitors from other parts of the city. People who
had been here Sunday night to see a show, have dinner, or
do some shopping, might not be here now. Probably
wouldn't be. Yet Ferdi had participated in other searches
with less to go on and been successful. Results depended on
dogged determination and meticulous attention to detail.

The last doorbell to be rung, the final witness to be interviewed, could provide the clue that would break the case.

Before laying out the grid and making the assignments, Ferdi had to determine whether the kidnapper had acted alone or with an accomplice. Discussing it with Norah, they had agreed the intruder had been alone. Two men would not have had any trouble subduing the aged actress. She would not have been able to put up the kind of resistance indicated by the condition of the apartment and her own state. But how about the boy? How had the kidnapper handled a sturdy and resourceful ten-year-old? He had to be taken out of the building and into the street without creating a disturbance. And then what? What were the getaway plans?

A car would have been parked near the service exit, Ferdi and Norah had reasoned. The boy would have been dragged or carried across the sidewalk. Kicking and screaming? Or drugged? An unconscious ten-year-old wouldn't be that easy to carry and would certainly attract attention. In some way he had been forced or convinced to cooperate. The fact remained that he was in his pajamas, and despite tolerance of weird getups, people would have been likely to notice a child on the street in pajamas—after midnight.

They agreed the kidnapper had acted alone in the apartment.

"But we know he had an accomplice in picking up the ransom," Norah pointed out. "Why didn't they act together from the beginning?"

"Maybe he didn't think he'd be needing an accomplice," Ferdi suggested. "Not according to the original plan. But then things started to go wrong. Wilma turned out to be a lot more trouble than he'd anticipated. So did the boy. When he found out that Wilma was dead and he'd be dealing with Adele Millard, he had to improvise."

They were both silent.

"It's possible the driver of the car didn't know about the kidnapping or the ransom," Ferdi went on. "Maybe the perp' asked a friend to do him a favor. Told him he had to be somewhere fast and that he needed a ride."

Norah was skeptical. "He would have had to come up with a pretty good reason for that fast getaway."

It was decided that for the time being they would proceed on the premise that the kidnapper had acted alone in the apartment and subsequently that night on the street.

Wilma Danay's building was on a quiet residential block between Second and Third Avenues. Someone passing might have noticed the man and boy. Ferdi assigned Neel and two detectives to question the doormen on both sides. Activity on the avenues continued through most of the night and into early morning. So Ferdi assigned the remaining four teams—the most he'd been able to muster—to check the video stores, supermarkets, fast-food joints, movie theaters, restaurants. They wakened the homeless curled up on the hot-air grates. Nobody had seen a man and child behaving in an unusual manner. The detectives had no photograph to show, nothing but the general description of the child, but they kept at it. By five in the morning they'd covered those businesses that stayed open for twenty-four hours; the others had long since closed. Arenas decided to call it off; further overtime wasn't warranted. He would resume later with a fresh crew.

By eight A.M., Arenas had assembled a force of fifty detectives, officer-investigators, and uniforms. He had decided to cover the side streets from First Avenue over to Lexington, and the avenues from Sixty-second to Sixty-eighth. It wasn't likely the kidnapper had parked any farther than that. If for any reason it should be deemed necessary to push out the parameters, he'd have to request more men. But at eight-

fifty-five, the team of Brody and Webber made that unnecessary.

"I didn't see it myself, Officers," the doorman of the
building at Sixty-third and Third explained. "Tony Sabbatini, the night watchman, told me."

"Is he still on the premises?" Brody didn't waste any time.

"Probably."

"When found, the night watchman, who had already
changed out of uniform and was anxious to go home,
wanted to make sure the officers understood. "I got the story
from one of the tenants, Mr. Lehr."

"We understand. Go on," Brody urged.

Sabbatini's bald pate glistened; he shifted uneasily. "It's
like this. After midnight we lock the doors and the tenant has
to·either use his key or ring the bell to be admitted. Mr. Lehr
had forgotten his key, so he rang. I opened up for him. He
was . . . not agitated, I wouldn't call it that, but concerned.
Troubled."

The watchman addressed himself to Sean Brody, the veteran, rather than to Kathryn Webber, the rookie, who was
too young and too pretty to inspire confidence in a man his
age. "He'd seen a child, a boy, out on the street struggling
against a man. The kid was trying to get loose and the man
was trying to hold on to him. Finally, the kid managed to free
himself and ran. The man yelled for help. He yelled that the
kid had his wallet and somebody should stop him. By that
time the kid was around the corner and gone. Nothing Mr.
Lehr could have done anyway. He's an elderly gentleman,"
Sabbatini told them.

Brody pursed his lips. "Did he report the incident?"

"Not as far as I know."

"You didn't think of reporting it?"

"No. I got the story secondhand. I told you that."

"You did."

Sabbatini shrugged. "By then both of them were long gone. What use would it have been?"

"That's for us to decide, not you," Kathryn Webber put in. "As it turns out, you could have saved us eight hours of asking questions."

Sabbatini started to retort, but at the look in her eyes he changed his mind. "Anything else?" he asked Brody.

Brody, not trusting himself to speak, shook his head. Finished with the night watchman, he got the witness's apartment number from the manager. Told that Conrad Lehr, a retired stock broker, was likely to be at home, he contacted Sergeant Arenas.

"Aren't we going to interrogate the witness?" Kathryn Webber asked. Her eyes were bright with excitement.

"That's the sergeant's job."

"But . . . we're the ones who turned him. Isn't it up to us to verify the story?"

"You know the answer to that. What did they teach you at the Academy?" Brody looked hard at his new partner. "Relax, Webber. Your time will come."

Kathryn flushed and said no more. She remained in the background while Brody made his report briefly and concisely.

"Good work, Sean," Arenas said. He regarded Kathryn. "Is this your first special assignment, Officer Webber?"

"Yes, sir."

"Good work."

She bit her lip. "Actually, it was Officer Brody who uncovered the lead. I just tagged along."

Arenas regarded her approvingly. "Sean Brody is an experienced officer. You couldn't have a better role model. Watch him and you'll learn a lot."

"I already have, sir."

With another nod, Arenas headed for the elevators.

Upstairs, Conrad Lehr was waiting.

He was tall, thin, a distinguished-looking man surely well into his eighties, Ferdi judged. He was very frail, and as the night watchman had indicated to the two uniforms, he would not have been physically capable of intervening between the alleged kidnapper and the boy. Lehr welcomed Arenas.

"I should have reported the incident right away," he berated himself as he led the way into the living room. It was long and narrow and made to seem more so by the arrangement of furniture along the two main walls. On a traditional, tooled leather-topped coffee table were a pair of heavy crystal ashtrays and a fine Jenssen's silver cigarette box, otherwise nothing else that might serve as ornamental. The drapes on the windows were damask, discolored by years of sun and musty with dust. Ferdi had been married long enough to recognize that no woman lived here. A tinted, but faded, wedding picture on the mantel indicated Conrad Lehr had not always been alone.

"I should have called 911." He went on reproaching himself. "I was tired. One sees so many things, terrible things, and there's nothing one can do . . . so one walks away." Lehr sighed. "It's wrong. We've got to take responsibility, personal responsibility, and we've got to start doing it now."

"Yes, sir," Arenas replied. "So if you could just tell me what happened?"

"Of course. Of course, I've delayed long enough." With a shaking hand he reached for a cigarette from the silver box. "I was coming home from the theater. It was one of those marathon productions that start early and run late. I couldn't get a taxi, so I walked to Fifty-seventh and then had to wait for the crosstown bus. Anyway, when I finally got here, the door was locked and I'd forgotten my key. It was one of those nights." He took a deep drag on the cigarette. "I was nervous waiting for Tony to come and let me in. I kept looking over my shoulder to make sure nobody was loitering. It's a damn shame. Once upon a time this was a safe neighborhood. Now there's no such thing. You're afraid of being mugged at your own front door.

"Anyway, I saw this man down the street about halfway. I can't give you a description, Sergeant; he was too far away and the trees still have enough leaves to blot out the street lights. I can say he was a big man, but that's about it."

Arenas was disappointed but not discouraged. "What about the boy?"

"He was a ball of fury, I can tell you that. He was kicking, biting, scratching. He left his mark on that man, you can be sure."

Arenas made a note in his book and underscored it. "Anything else? Have you any idea how old the child was?" Lehr shook his head. "Could you make out how he was dressed?"

"Of course, of course," the old man groaned. "I'm so forgetful lately. I can't remember the simplest thing. I go to the store and I have no idea what I went to buy. I didn't think getting old would be like this." He looked at the photograph on the mantel. "Sometimes I think Emily was fortunate. She had the best of it."

"You were going to tell me how the boy was dressed," Arenas recalled gently.

"Yes, yes. He was in pajamas. At least, that's what it looked like. It might have been a jogging outfit. Though I don't know what a young child would be doing out jogging in the middle of the night any more than why he would be out in pajamas."

Once more he lost himself, and Ferdi had to prompt. "Then what happened?"

"Ah, well, the boy managed to get loose and ran toward

Third. The man chased him. They turned the corner and that's the last I saw of either one of them. I don't know whether the man caught him or not, but based on their relative speed—I'd say no."

"I'd say there's a strong possibility that Todd Millard got away." Ferdi Arenas concluded his report.

Norah nodded and looked around her office at the detectives gathered there. Along with Arenas, she had called in Neel, Wyler, and Ochs, the men she most relied on. She let them see her relief, knowing they shared it. For a few moments at least the heavy anxiety was eased.

"It would explain why the kidnapper was so quick to make his ransom demand and why it was so relatively modest," Norah pointed out. "It also explains why he agreed to accept what was offered. He couldn't afford to wait; he didn't have the boy. In all probability, he never did."

The satisfaction, however, was fleeting.

"So, if Todd got away, where is he now?" she asked and the question hung ominously over them. "Why hasn't he turned up?"

Chapter

ELEVEN

The first thing Norah had to do was notify the parents. While she regarded the new development with strong optimism, it was not the kind of news to impart over the telephone. She decided to go directly to Wilma Danay's apartment. As she'd expected, Adele Millard was still there, still in the library, close to the telephone.

From the time she had received the message in Chicago on Monday morning informing her of her son's disappearance, Adele Millard had been hit with one shock after other. Returning to New York, she learned of her mother's death and moments after she'd absorbed that, she was told it was murder. Next, the kidnapper made his demand. She raised the money and had the courage and stamina to deliver it only to bear the dreadful realization that the boy would not be returned and contact with the kidnapper was lost.

It was no wonder she showed every minute of those thirty-six hours, Norah thought. She was gray and drawn. Lines etched deep. Lips cracked. Hair hanging lank with the sweat of despair.

Norah hesitated about raising her hopes. If the hope turned out to be false, could she handle another disappointment? Norah decided not to give any slant to the account but to tell it simply and straight out.

"We have reason to believe Todd got away from his kidnapper."

She didn't seem to take it in. "How do you mean—got away? Where is he?"

"We thought you might have some idea." Norah paused, then went on to explain. "He wouldn't have gone home because he knew you weren't there. His father lives in Connecticut, and he didn't have the money to call for him to come and get him."

"Richard and Louise were away too. Oh God, poor Todd." She put a hand over her eyes to hide her tears. Apparently, the possibility that Millard might be behind the attempted kidnapping didn't even occur to her.

"So even if he'd somehow managed to place the call, he wouldn't have got an answer," Norah concluded. "By the way, where is Professor Millard now?"

"Back with his wife. She's due to give birth any day."

"How does Todd feel about his father's wife?"

"They get along, I guess."

And she resented that they did, Norah thought, but that was natural. "Is there somewhere else Todd might have gone? Anyone else to whom he might turn—school friends, teachers?"

"No. Todd was . . . is . . . an outgoing child, but he didn't . . . doesn't make friends easily. Oh my God!"

"Easy. Take it easy, Mrs. Millard. We're dealing with a missing or possibly lost child now rather than one who is being forcibly detained, and that improves our odds considerably." Briskly, in a matter-of-fact manner, Norah outlined the steps that would be taken, not asking for cooperation but taking it for granted. "The first thing we need is a recent photograph; the ones I've seen go back a couple of years."

"I'm sure we can find some recent snapshots. My mother was a big camera buff and Todd was her favorite subject. Yolanda will know."

Yolanda Yates was called.

"Hello, Lieutenant. Good to see you." Her look was friendly and her words certainly indicated that she bore no grudge against Norah for having been excluded from the negotiations with the kidnapper. She was eager to help and produced a stack of albums filled largely with photographs of the missing boy. Norah selected one of the most recent.

"Now, we know he was wearing pajamas. Has either of you any idea what color?" she asked.

As before, the mother didn't know, but the companion did. "Wilma bought him several pairs, which were kept here in his bureau. The ones that are missing are navy with red ribbing at the ankles and wrists. They could pass for a jogging outfit."

"Ah." Norah made a note. "How about bedroom slippers or shoes?"

A diligent search didn't turn up slippers in the boy's closet, not under his bed, nor in the bathroom.

"So he must have been wearing them," Norah concluded. "All right. We'll have flyers made up with this picture and a description. They'll be distributed locally and at airports and bus terminals. We'll flood the neighborhood with detectives. We'll search out hiding places." In a small town, everybody would join in the search, Norah thought. Here, in this big, impersonal, cynical city, it was not any different when the heart was touched.

"Remember that ninety percent of lost children are found alive, Mrs. Millard. Hold on to that thought."

Adele Millard was not reassured, and though Yolanda Yates offered comfort as usual, it seemed to Norah that both women had reached the same conclusion she had—that

Todd was not captive and not lost. He was afraid and hiding. And that would make him a lot more difficult to find.

There were places where runaways congregated. Norah put out the word to her informants, and then, impatient, went to look herself. Working on the business of the squad by day, she spent the nights at the juvenile centers.

She hadn't realized there were so many: government-run, supported by religious groups, privately financed. So many children passed through them—lost, abandoned. Frightened, rebellious.

She met with varying attitudes from those in charge, from compassionate to sullen and resentful, but they had to acknowledge her authority. Not the children. They recognized her as a cop, and even the very young ones had learned to be wary. Nevertheless, she wandered among them looking into their faces, asking—though she got no answer. One night, two, three, till she was certain Todd was not there. It was time to move on, to go where the children went to sustain themselves in the only way they could, by selling the only merchandise they had. It was time to hit the streets. Norah started with the Minnesota Strip.

It is a stretch of approximately fifteen blocks along Eighth Avenue parallel to Times Square and bordering what is known as the *legitimate* theater. It is comprised of porno houses, cheap bars, strip joints, pizza parlors. Overhead, the light of their marquees beckon in tawdry brilliance. Underfoot, the street is littered with trash, and garbage cans overflow. Prostitutes, male and female, flaunt their wares. Drunks, addicts, and the homeless mix with affluent theatergoers who drift over from the shows that charge a hundred dollars a ticket.

There were plenty of uniforms around, Norah noted, but they couldn't begin to clear out the traffickers and their human merchandise. They were a presence merely, to prevent the seething pot from boiling over. It was the best they could do. As at the shelters, Norah walked among the children, looked into their old faces, and when one of them appeared a little less angry or a little less apathetic, she showed Todd's picture. No one had seen him, or would admit it.

Norah had worked Homicide for over ten years, but the squalor and degradation that was a regular part of these children's lives was almost more than she could bear. Yet she went back, night after night, to the strip and to other foul pockets of the city. But now her hope was that Todd would not be *here*.

Then on Monday, November nineteenth, another woman went off the platform at the Fifty-ninth Street and Lexington Avenue subway station.

Helen Wyatt shouldn't have been on that platform at all. She should have gotten off a stop ahead, but she'd missed it. She was a stranger in New York, uncertain of her way, and by the time she realized she was at her station and should be getting off, the doors were closing. The car was jammed and she couldn't make her way through.

She'd been daydreaming. Ever since the letter inviting her to New York for an interview had come, she'd been in a lovely daze. Helen Wyatt was twenty-three, filled with idealism and determined to make her mark, to count for something. College was not fulfilling; campus life seemed an artificial environment, but her parents would not countenance her dropping out to do nothing. Nor was she inclined to that. Then she met Lesley Dorenmann. He had spent four years with the World Health Organization in Africa and after a short home leave, was going back. His stories excited her. She was wild to go, too. Her parents were skeptical, not to say opposed. They were upper middle-class people and their only child had been given all the advantages within their means and aspirations. Helen was a beautiful girl, fair skinned and dark haired. She'd been given ballet lessons, piano lessons, learned to ride and had her own horse. She had studied in Paris for a year and spoke French well. They had thought she might choose a career in the arts or teaching. They consoled themselves that a tour of duty with the WHO did not constitute a permanent commitment.

In the old-fashioned sense, Helen Wyatt had been "gently reared." How could she handle life in a mud hut, without sanitary facilities, subsisting on a diet they shuddered to contemplate? Was her eagerness sparked by this young man, Lesley Dorenmann? Was he, rather than WHO, the real attraction? Helen was basically a sensible girl, but she could be stubborn. With or without their blessing, the Wyatts knew she would go. Best give it to her.

Everett and Mary Wyatt weren't too happy for their only child to be spending the weekend in New York City on her own, either, but having agreed that she could go to a third-world country for two years, they could hardly forbid her two days less than a hundred miles from home. They worried about what would happen between her and her young man, if it hadn't happened already.

It hadn't. Helen had every expectation and anticipation that it would, sooner or later. For now, she was interested only in being accepted by the WHO. Lesley had promised to coach her for the coming interview. He had the use of a friend's apartment on West Fifty-eighth Street, and she was on her way to meet him there.

The train hurtled on, yet it seemed to Helen Wyatt that it would never get to the next station. She'd learned one lesson, however, and that was to be near the door so that when it did stop, she'd be able to get off. As a result, she was almost catapulted out to the platform.

"Downtown? Please, how do I get a downtown train?" she

asked over and over. Finally a woman with a child in a stroller took the trouble to point across the platform. "Read the sign."

Downtown and Brooklyn R and N Trains

"Thank you," Helen said, embarrassed she hadn't seen for herself, but the woman was already gone, part of the tide surging toward the escalator. So Helen waited. After three trains had come and gone on the uptown side, she began to wonder why nothing was coming in on her side. Was there a problem? She'd heard that New York subways were totally unreliable; something was always going wrong; power was always being cut off for one reason or another. She stepped to the edge of the platform to peer into the tunnel. Nothing. While she looked, she had a prickly feeling at her back, the sense of being watched.

Instantly, she drew back.

There was a homeless man about three feet from her. He was a bundle of rags held together by a rope around his waist. It struck her that his legs—what she could see of them through the tears in his pants—were white and clean. She looked up. Their eyes met. His were gray-blue and looked lighter because of the encrusted dirt on his face. She looked quickly away. *Never make eye contact;* she'd heard that some-where. Then she was ashamed. He was a poor, unfortunate man and she should feel sorry for him, not afraid.

But he continued to stare at her. She edged away and he followed, getting closer. *Where was the train? Why didn't the train come?* It was getting late and she didn't want to keep Lesley waiting. Maybe she should go up to the street and try to get a cab?

Then she heard it—a low rumble in the distance. At last. As she lined up to get on, she noticed he was doing the same. Well, why not? Let him get on. She was going to ride for one stop. What could happen?

The rumble grew louder. She leaned forward, craning her

neck to see. Yes, there was the train headlight growing brighter as it came closer to the station. Brighter and brighter . . .

She felt a shove in the upper part of her back. She pitched forward.

"It's the third time," Transit Police Chief Benjamin Woitach pointed out, exercising considerable restraint. "It's the third time since October fifteenth that a woman has been run over and killed at that same station."

Charles Aspen, his head of detectives, knew only too well the reasonable tone masked grave concern. "People have been falling, jumping, or being pushed to the tracks in stations all over the system. Sooner or later we were bound to have a repeat."

The discussion was taking place at their regular Tuesday morning breakfast meeting in the chief's office at Transit Police Headquarters on Jay Street in downtown Brooklyn.

Benjamin Woitach was a crusader. He had a reputation for reorganizing to improve the productivity of any department he headed. He was also known for lifting morale, for instilling pride in the job in his people. Thirty-eight years old, he was young for his present position, but he came to it with a history of achievement in like situations. He had reshaped and strengthened state police agencies in Pennsylvania and Rhode Island. The job he faced now was tougher than either.

For years the 3,700-member New York City Transit Department Police was looked down upon by the public and the 26,000 members of the city force. Worse, by its own members. While all cadets trained together, it was the luck of the draw which were assigned to the regular force, to transit, or to the housing corp. Nobody wanted to be sent down *into the hole, the electric sewer.* Nobody wanted to be called *tunnel rat* or *subway mouse.*

Woitach was married and he had four children all under the age of twelve. His wife was a school teacher. They both rode the subway to work. He spent the first month on the job learning the operations of the transit system and after that the crime pattern and statistics. He had a map drawn up of the high-incidence locations. He studied response time and solution rate. One thing was glaringly evident and disturbing: his force, the Transit Police, rarely handled high-profile assignments. These went almost, as a matter of course, to the police above ground.

"A repeat?" Woitach asked.

Aspen knew he had made a mistake.

"We have three victims: female." The chief reviewed the situation. "Each: Caucasian, single, medium height, dark hair. Each died on the tracks of the same station at between five-twenty and five-fifty-one P.M.: the height of the after-noon rush hour." He paused for emphasis. "And each one on the same day of the week."

"There are a lot of weirdos loose in this city on the streets and under them."

"You think it's a coincidence?" Woitach was grim.

Aspen was starting to sweat. A cigarette would have helped, but the chief didn't allow smoking in his office. Charles Aspen had come from the city force. After twenty-three years, having reached the rank of inspector, he saw further rise blocked by the change of administration. The new mayor brought in a new PC and the new man in turn brought in his own people. In fact, Aspen had actively backed the man who had lost the race for the job. He had gambled and lost. He was out. Before being demoted or assigned to some outpost, he had resigned, thinking he'd have no difficulty in getting a high-paying security job in private industry. It hadn't happened. He was out of work for two years before he landed this present job on the transit force.

There was a lot of talk about merging the three departments: city, transit, and housing. Before the change in his fortunes, Aspen had been in favor, but Ben Woitach was opposed and naturally he backed his new chief. Woitach thought merging was, in actuality, absorption. The way to avoid it was to strengthen the efficiency of the smaller force and make it an effective, specialized unit. The first step to achieving that was to raise morale. Woitach provided new and up-to-date equipment, including semiautomatic weapons. He meant to see to it that the *cops in the hole* got a fair share of the homicides, rapes, and shootouts that presently were caught by the cops on top.

Aspen opened the file folder he'd brought with him. "The first incident, the fall of Thelma Harrison to the tracks, was deemed an accident. The next two could be copy-cat crimes."

"Do you honestly believe that's what they are?" Ben Woitach asked. "The media isn't going to buy that. Neither is the public. And I don't want them to." He scowled. "My God, Charlie, if the passenger gets the idea that every time he goes down those steps and stands on a subway platform he's at risk, he's going to stop going down. He's going to stop using the subway. Then what? Ridership has already dropped."

"A serial killer?" Aspen put it out cautiously.

"Is that your other choice, a serial killer?"

"Eliminating accidents or suicides, what else? But if we announce a serial killer, I don't see it's going to reassure the public."

"It will when we catch him." Woitach fixed his chief of detectives with a steady stare.

So that was it, Aspen thought; the chief saw in these deaths an opportunity to prove that the transit force was capable of more than combating fare evasion and disorderly conduct. By solving a complex crime, he would dramatize the ability of the transit cops to protect the public and police their own turf.

Charlie Aspen was no longer young. Though he worked out in the gym every day and dyed his hair and watched his weight, he wasn't fooling anybody. If this job didn't pan out . . .

"We will get him, won't we?" Woitach demanded.

Aspen was sweating profusely. "I've got my best man on it. Dave Juvelis."

"He's good, is he?"

"The best I've got."

"He'll have to work with whoever they assign."

Aspen knew who *they* meant.

"Fine."

Actually, he was relieved. It would be a pilot project, he thought. If the case was cleared, there would be enough glory to go around. If it wasn't, the blame could be shared. A no-lose situation.

On Wednesday morning Manny Jacoby called Lieutenant Mulcahaney into his office and gave her the news.

She didn't know what to say.

"You're surprised, understandably."

"That's putting it mildly, Captain."

"You should feel complimented."

"I do, yes, of course, but I've got my hands full. We've barely scratched the surface of the Danay case."

"I thought you were well along."

"No, sir. And we're still searching for the boy, for Todd Millard."

"So we call in the FBI."

"Mrs. Millard doesn't want them. But I put out feelers anyway," Norah said. "They're not keen. They say we waited too long. That we botched it. And they're not interested in cleaning up our mess."

Jacoby scowled. "They don't have any choice in the matter. I'll see to it . . ."

"They think they're punishing us, Captain, but actually they're doing us a favor. I want to stay on the case, Captain. I want to get that boy back."

"Who said anything about taking you off? This subway thing needn't be full-time. Think of it as a consulting job. Their man, David Juvelis, is carrying. He's been informed you're going to . . . uh . . . work with him. So, talk it over. Give him your ideas, and let him do the legwork."

"He's going to love that," Norah said.

Manny Jacoby shrugged and waved her off as he reached for the telephone.

Chapter

TWELVE

Norah telephoned Detective Juvelis, introduced herself, and suggested they would do well to get acquainted. She would be in his neighborhood around eleven; would that be a convenient time for her to drop by? She could quite properly have asked him to come to her office, but she wanted to avoid any appearance of trying to take over. He sounded surprised that she would go to him, but not mollified.

It was not the first time Norah had walked into a strange squad room and introduced herself to a police officer who might be inclined to resent her. It had never been easy and she didn't anticipate it would be this time. There was the added friction of belonging to different and rival services. Norah decided to be direct and up front about the situation.

Having had Juvelis pointed out to her, she marched up to his desk and thrust out her hand. "Hello. I'm Norah Mulcahaney." For a moment she thought he wasn't going to respond. Then, slowly, he got to his feet and reached across the desk.

"David Juvelis."

"I don't suppose you're particularly thrilled to see me."

It took a moment for him to decide how to reply. "No, not particularly."

"I'm not thrilled to be here," she told him.

He was strikingly handsome. Tall, at least six-three; his bronze skin suggested a recent trip south or a sun lamp. He was also young, around twenty-five. He reminded Norah that on the twenty-eighth of this month she would be forty and that youth was no longer one of her assets. To him she must be in the same category as a school teacher or a maiden aunt. She almost sighed aloud.

"I don't want to step on your toes and I certainly don't want to take over your investigation. Okay? I've got my own problems."

He nodded, but he was still unconvinced.

"Why don't we try to make the best of it and work together? The sooner we get the job done, the sooner we'll be out of each other's hair."

"Sure." He waved her to the chair beside his desk and then sat himself.

Norah got down to business. "I've read your report. The similarities in the three incidents are glaring. The time, the place, the manner of death match. The victims are of an age and moderately good-looking. Have you been able to find any link between them?"

"Not yet. Harrison was a nurse, Christie a cocktail waitress, and Wyatt was in town for an interview with the World Health Organization. Harrison and Wyatt lived in the east sixties and Wyatt was staying at the Barbizon on Lex'. The only link is that they used the same subway station."

"Regularly?"

"Harrison and Christie—yes, to get to and from work."

"They both worked at night?"

"Right. Except for Wyatt, of course, who was a transient."

"That's interesting."

Juvelis shrugged.

"So it wasn't a matter of the first two just happening to be out at that hour on a Monday?"

"No."

"So then why did he kill on Monday? Monday appears to have had no special significance for the victims." Norah was careful not to imply that he had not reasoned this out. "If we accept that the time and the place are *no* coincidence, then we can't say that the day *is* a coincidence. It has to have significance and the significance has to apply to the perpetrator."

"You mean maybe the perp' only used the subway, or that particular station, on that particular day of the week?" The sharp way he looked at Norah belied the casual tone. David Juvelis was reassessing Lieutenant Mulcahaney.

"That's one possibility. Getting back to the victims; they were all three single, right? Harrison lived alone. Christie had a roommate, and Wyatt was on her own in a hotel. How about boyfriends?"

"Wyatt had a boyfriend. He set up the interview with WHO. Where's this heading, Lieutenant?"

"I'm floundering," Norah admitted. "I'm looking for a motive. Why were these women killed? Why were they killed in this particular way, pushed off that particular subway platform, on that particular day of the week? We have to search into their past."

"Excuse me, Lieutenant, but what the hell do you think we've been doing? We're not amateurs here."

"I'm sorry. I didn't mean . . ."

"The women came from small towns and were just beginning to establish a life here and a network of connections. Harrison was here the longest, close to two years. She was a nurse and more involved in the community than the others, but still without real roots. Christie, the waitress, was here over a year and in that time held three different jobs before settling in at The Village Café. We've talked to the doctors and staff at St. Vincent's where Harrison worked part time. She was well liked, got along with everybody. Was not known to have a steady boyfriend or outside interests. Same goes for Christie."

"How about Harrison's patients?" Norah asked. "Did you talk to them? And Christie's customers? They couldn't all have loved her. Didn't she ever spill the drinks? Or bring the wrong order? Why did she leave the other three jobs?"

For answer, David Juvelis opened the top left-hand drawer of his desk and took out a thick file folder and placed it in front of Norah. "If you think you can do better, Lieutenant, be my guest."

"I told you before, it's your case. But I have to point out to you that pressure on the killer is mounting. The first murder—that's right, *murder;* let's forget accident and suicide and call it what it is—took place on Monday, October fifteenth. The second was on November twelfth, a month later, and the third, on November nineteenth, just a week after. If that's a pattern, and I believe it is, another woman will be pushed to the tracks at that station this coming Monday."

"God, Lieutenant! I've got three men working the case with me. To trace every patient Thelma Harrison attended during the past two years and every customer Christie served and then interrogate each one . . . I couldn't do it with thirty."

"Have you asked for them?"

"Hell, no."

"Ask. Ask for fifty. You'll get them."

"Isn't that up to you?"

Norah considered. "You're right." Her blue eyes narrowed and she clenched her jaw. Then she took a deep breath and expelled it slowly. "We'll take our fifty men and throw them all into the Harrison investigation. She was the first victim and, logically, she's the key. Somewhere in her past we'll find the connection, not to the other victims but to the killer. Sometime in the past, Thelma Harrison and the killer collided. Something happened. I don't know what, but it got her killed. We'll concentrate our force on her every known relationship, personal and professional. It's a gamble, but I believe the odds are in our favor."

Manny Jacoby was skeptical.

Not that Norah had expected him to be anything else, and anyway the request for a task force of that size had to be referred up the chain of command. But he agreed to do that much and she was counting on the public relations aspect of the situation to sell her idea to the brass. Norah had consulted a police psychologist and he supported her theory that the killer could be expected to follow the one-week timetable. If he did and another woman died under a train this next Monday, at least both the Transit Police and NYPD could say they had not stinted on men or money.

Of course, Norah didn't expect to be at the head of such a force; the command would go to someone of higher rank. She was right; Jim Felix took over for NYPD and Charles Aspen for the Transit Police. However, when it got down to the nuts and bolts, it was Norah Mulcahaney and David Juvelis who ran the operation. Using Thelma Harrison's employment file at St. Vincent's, they set up those to be questioned, made the assignments, studied the reports, all, at Norah's insistence, from Transit offices.

The first break came quickly. While Harrison worked part-time at the hospital, she also worked out of a nurse's registry and took private patients. No one had mentioned that the first time around, Juvelis claimed. At Norah's look, he modified the statement.

"Maybe it was mentioned and didn't seem important." He cleared his throat. "When Harrison was killed, back in October, she was the first, so we figured it was probably an accident, or, at the worst, a random killing. There didn't seem to be any need to dig deeper."

Norah nodded.

"The next time, November twelfth, when Joanna Christie died, we did note the similarities, of course, but . . . two victims don't constitute a series." He paused. "Now we've got a third, but still no connection."

"We'll find it. That's what we've got the task force for."

The next day was Thanksgiving; most offices would be closed. Usually Norah had the holiday dinner with Joe's family at his mother's place in Brooklyn. She saw no reason to cancel, but on Friday she met Juvelis in the morning and together they visited the nurse's registry. They searched through Thelma Harrison's employment file. During the two-year period she'd been in New York, Harrison had attended two hundred and forty-one private patients, some in the hospital and some in their own homes. Norah and Juvelis divided them up among the force. It came to about five patients per investigator. They were to interrogate not only the patient but family and friends, digging for any *unusual occurrence,* no matter how minor or irrelevant it might seem. The detectives worked diligently; overtime was authorized, but the days slipped away and Monday loomed ominously.

On the advice of the police psychiatrist, the investigation was handled quietly for fear of stimulating the killer, rousing him, perhaps causing him to panic and to act before he'd intended—in other words, speed up his timetable. A round-the-clock watch was put on the lower platform of the Lexington Avenue and Fifty-ninth Street station over the weekend, just in case. However, it was not thought likely the perp' would risk revealing himself without the cover provided by the weekday crowds. Meantime, preparation for a full stake-out on Monday was under way.

The Tactical Squad was called in, expert marksmen skilled in crowd control. Plainclothes cops, men and women in various guises—businessmen, laborers, students—would mix with the crowd on the platform, keeping an eye on every young, dark-haired woman who was alone. At the first indication of a possible assault, the officer nearest the intended victim was to intervene. At all costs, the victim must be protected; her safety was the top priority. While the first officer moved to avert the attack, all others would converge to collar the perp'. At a signal, the guards above ground would seal off the exits to the street.

Norah was skeptical. "What if he's armed?"

"He's never used weapons," Juvelis pointed out.

"Which doesn't mean he's not carrying," Norah retorted.

She would have liked to know more about how the killer chose his victims. The first two, Harrison and Christie, used the station regularly. Was there a significance in that? Did he observe them for a while before the attack? Stalk them? Helen Wyatt was from out of town; obviously he'd had no opportunity to observe her habits. Why had she been chosen?

All of this distracted Norah from the Danay case. Then Wyler informed her that Jerome Ritter, Wilma Danay's lawyer, had returned. She'd planned to interview him herself, but there simply was no time. She sent Wyler and Arenas instead. More than anything, she was troubled because she had to suspend her personal search for Todd Millard. She promised herself that after the stakeout she would ask to be relieved of her part in the subway killings investigation. She waited anxiously for Monday to come around.

The force started moving in at four—singly, in pairs, in groups. They were positioned on the lower platform, but some were also posted at the upper in case he varied his m.o., or to head off a possible escape attempt on one of the trains at that level. A sharp-shooter, rifle at the ready, hid in the token booth. At four-thirty, when Norah Mulcahaney and David Juvelis arrived, everyone was in place. By five P.M., regular riders crowded the upper and lower platforms with a steady stream going up and down the escalators. Among them Norah spotted a familiar face. She was one of a group of three girls wearing the green plaid skirt and dark green blazer of St. Vincent Ferrer school.

Kathryn Webber.

Their eyes met for a fleeting moment and it was Norah who looked away.

What was Sally Felix's niece doing here? She was too new, too inexperienced. She could throw a spanner into the whole operation; at best, she was useless and taking the place of a proven professional. Whom had she conned to get the assignment? Norah intended to find out.

Seeing Kathryn in the school uniform took Norah back to her own early days on the force. She'd spent the whole first year mostly on matron duties. She'd hated it. At that time, her whole effort had been directed toward getting posted to a precinct and real police work. While still working out of the pool, she'd been sent to search the body of a female victim, the closest she'd come to an actual investigation. There, she caught the attention of Joe Capretto, then a sergeant. He was working on a series of murders of young widows and he requested Norah Mulcahaney for decoy duty. Times hadn't changed that much for women in the department, Norah thought. It still wasn't easy to be accepted on the basis of ability. Why should she blame Kathryn Webber for using what means she could to get ahead? It was possible that Jim Felix himself had gotten her this job. He had helped Norah many times. The difference was that Kathryn was related to the three-star chief whereas Norah had had to earn his attention and support.

Remembering the bright gleam in Webber's eyes when they met hers, and the quick rise of color in her cheeks,

Norah interpreted them as excitement and also embarrassment. The girl had sensed Norah's resentment at her presence, but she couldn't know the reason for it. Till this moment, Norah herself hadn't known why she felt as she did. Very simply, it was Kathryn Webber's youth. Kathryn stood at the threshold of her career with opportunity ahead. She was looking forward; Norah was looking back.

Resolutely, Norah turned away from the rookie and focused her attention on the milling crowd. The trains were roaring by, in and out of the station, one after the other, at peak-hour frequency. Passengers had to shove to get off while those on the platform pushed to get on. It was the headroom, the time between trains, that was dangerous, and Norah noticed that most people were keeping well back from the edge of the platform. They were dependent on the subways, but they were afraid. Strangers pressed up against each other yet managed to avoid psychological contact. *No man is an island,* Norah thought, yet here, in this city, every man wished to be.

She paid most attention to the young women, those in their mid-twenties, dark-haired, who might qualify as the next victim. There was one standing right at the edge. Norah felt a tremendous desire to go over and caution her, but, of course, she couldn't. All she could do was hold her breath as the girl leaned out to look into the tunnel while a homeless man shambled toward her. Norah was poised. One more step and she would have tackled him and brought him down.

At that moment, whether she sensed danger or not, the young woman stepped back. The vagrant shuffled away. The R train bound for Queens entered the station and screeched to a halt.

Norah spotted no more likely victims or suspects. By six-thirty, the crowd had thinned. She had no idea how many persons had passed through that station during the time period, but tonight, at least, they had done it safely. At seven P.M., the signal was given and as gradually and casually as it had assembled, the task force dispersed.

On the street, Norah caught up with Kathryn Webber. "Your first stakeout? What did you think of it?"

The rookie seemed surprised at being approached. "It was interesting."

"Interesting?" Norah repeated.

The girl took a deep breath. She came alive. "Actually, I thought it was exciting."

"Ah . . ." Norah nodded and smiled at Kathryn Webber. "I thought so, too, my first time."

Chapter

THIRTEEN

Nathaniel Gorin emerged from the subway at the Third Avenue exit badly shaken. He blinked in the waning daylight. It was the first time he'd encountered the slightest difficulty. Up to then everything had proceeded with an almost predestined smoothness that seemed to confirm the justice of his cause, not that he'd ever had any doubt. Today, well, he wasn't exactly sure what had happened. Dazed, he stood at the top of the subway steps, blocking the way, unaware that he was being jostled first to one side then the other as people tried to get by.

"Are you alive?"

A hard elbow into his side sent him stumbling to his knees off the sidewalk and into the gutter. No one put out a hand to catch him. On the contrary, people nearby jumped clear. A driver blew his horn, angry because he was forced to swerve to avoid hitting him.

The pain of the fall shocked Gorin back to reality. He picked himself up.

What had happened down there on the platform?

He had been standing in his usual position for about twenty minutes when he spotted her. He had plenty of time to observe her. She was the one all right, the one he'd been looking for: slim, medium height, dark hair and light eyes, and she was wearing a short red coat so that it was easy for him to follow her movements in the crowd. Which side of the platform would she choose—uptown and Queens or downtown and Brooklyn? She chose the uptown side and he was pleased; at this hour and at this level there were more people waiting there and it seemed the trains were more frequent. She took a position about halfway along the platform. Also good. The train would be slowing as it entered the station but would still be going too fast to stop in time. He started his move in her direction.

At the distant sound of the approaching train, she leaned out to take a look. Very good. Unexpectedly, she turned. They were close and for three or four seconds they looked directly at each other. In her face, he saw terror. It was what he wanted to see. In his face, she saw her fate. She knew what was going to happen. He smiled as he raised his hands palms forward—and stopped. He felt a strange sensation: eyes boring into his back; eyes all around him. He was being watched. He whirled, searching the faces. No one met his look.

The roar of the train grew louder. Gorin turned back to the woman.

She was gone.

The train pulled in. A crowd pushed to get out and another surge of people shoved to get in. Then he caught sight of the red coat one car down just as the doors shut with a pneumatic hiss.

Too late.

The sensation of being watched was gone. Nevertheless, he examined the people around him. Their faces were blank, anonymous. Had he imagined the whole thing? No, he had not. He knew the feeling. He'd had it the first time he'd been interviewed by the police a year ago. Were they watching him? Why? What could have put them on to him? Nothing. He had given all the right answers. There was nothing to worry about. Just the same, he'd have to be careful, extra careful from now on.

Why hadn't he acted?

That was the question everybody connected with the investigation of the subway murders and the abortive stakeout asked himself. Did the killer suspect he was being watched? Had he sensed the trap? Or was he in a quiescent period? If so, how long would it last? Was it possible he had achieved his purpose and no longer needed to kill? Was he through?

"We may never hear from him again," Norah said.

On the Tuesday morning after the failed stakeout, she had presented herself to Chief Felix in his office in the Big Building, One Police Plaza. "It's not as satisfying as catching him in the act, but as long as the subways are safe again . . . That was the purpose of the exercise."

"Or he might strike again next Monday," Felix suggested. "We've decided to continue the interrogation of Thelma Harrison's patients. After that, we'll start on the people who knew Joanna Christie."

"I'd like to get back to my regular work," Norah said. "You've got fifty men on this case, and I've only got my regular team on the Danay murder and kidnapping. *And* they have to cover the chart."

"I thought you had Arenas in charge?"

"I do, but . . ."

"You really believe the boy is still alive?" Felix asked gently. "It's been . . . how many days?"

"Fifteen," she replied without hesitation. "I know that's a long time and that with each day that passes the chances of getting him back diminish, but I don't think Todd is being held against his will. For one, there's been no further communication from the kidnapper, and two, a kidnapper isn't likely to hold on to the living evidence against him for this long.

"I think the boy got away and he's hiding. I don't know why. Maybe he's afraid to go home because the kidnapper is part of the family circle and if he names him, he won't be believed."

"So where is he? How is he surviving?" Felix pressed. "I assume you've had somebody check the juvenile facilities?"

"I went myself. I visited the shelters, I asked around on the street. I still have to check the Welfare family hotels. With so many kids running around loose in those places, who's going to notice one more or less?"

"And if he's not there?"

"I don't know. I'll go back to the streets. He's out there somewhere, alone and frightened. I know it." Norah's strong chin quivered for a moment. Then she set it. "I'm not giving up on him, Jim. I'm not."

Felix's green eyes, which were so like Kathryn Webber's, though she was related to his wife, not to him, reflected his sympathy. "You do what you have to do."

Once again Norah was in her office with Arenas and Wyler reporting on their session with Ritter.

"Danay left her entire estate, value unknown but estimated to be in the neighborhood of twelve million, to her grandson, Todd Millard. In trust, of course, till his eighteenth birthday."

Norah formed a silent whistle. Somehow, she hadn't been expecting the estate would be so large. It shouldn't surprise her, she decided, and waited for Ferdi to continue.

"Peter Bouchard is the executor but with strictures as to exactly how to administer the estate. An allowance for Todd and for his mother are specifically provided. Adjustments made for various stages of their lives, sums to be spent for daily needs, education, travel. In the event anything happens to Adele Millard and the boy goes to live with his father, the monies specified are to devolve on Richard Millard."

"Interesting."

Ferdi nodded. "There are other bequests: certain paintings to Peter Bouchard; items of jewelry including a cabochon emerald ring given to Danay by her second husband, Quentin Noble, to go to Camilla Bouchard."

"There doesn't seem to have been any jealousy between the two women," Norah observed.

"I don't know whether that means neither cares all that much about Bouchard, but it's a little too modern for me," Ferdi remarked.

"Anything else?"

"A million dollars to Nicholas Kouriades to produce a certain script they'd been discussing."

"Wow! And the companion, Yolanda Yates?"

"Twenty-five thousand plus the use of the apartment, maintenance paid, during her lifetime. The apartment is, of course, the property of Todd Millard. He can sell it if he wants but must provide her with lodging on a par."

"How about Richard Millard?"

"He's out of it unless, as I mentioned, Adele dies and the boy goes to live with him."

"And if the boy dies first?"

There was a moment of silence.

"The special bequests stand, but the capital goes to the Actors' Home in Jersey."

Norah considered. "Is it possible that what we're dealing with here is not a kidnapping but a murder? That the purpose was not to snatch the boy but to kill Wilma Danay for the inheritance?"

"Could be," Ferdi said.

"We've discussed it," Wyler put in. "Any one of the three regulars who played bridge at the Danay apartment that Sunday night could have come back after the game. All the person had to do was ring the bell and say he'd forgotten something. Danay would have let him in without question." He paused. "On the other hand, the perp' went to the trouble of buying a pizza as an excuse to get into the building."

"The pizza was to get him past the doorman," Ferdi pointed out.

"But he was a regular. The doorman knew him and would have let him back up without question," Wyler objected.

"Exactly," Ferdi retorted with a gleam of triumph. "He would have let him up and he would have remembered letting him up. The perp' didn't want that."

Norah let them toss it around.

"If he was one of the Sunday-night regulars, he would have had to do more than carry a pizza in his hands to disguise his identity," Arenas said.

"We're arguing about nothing," Wyler concluded. "The doorman swears nobody from the Pizza Palace made a delivery that night. But supposing for the sake of argument, someone did try to get upstairs by pretending to deliver a pizza, the doorman would have called up and Danay would have told him she didn't order anything, and that would have been the end of that."

"All right, fine. It couldn't have happened, but it did," Ferdi said. "The perp' did gain entry, first to the building and then to the apartment. As there was no sign of force, she must have let him in. It didn't have to be one of the bridge players, but it was someone she knew. So, she opened the door, and when she saw him with the pizza she was confused. She hesitated just long enough for him to push in past her.

"At that moment, she realized something very bad was about to happen and she screamed and ran. He dropped the box and grabbed her to silence her. They struggled. She broke away, ran to the kitchen and got the knife. By this time they were making a lot of noise, furniture was being turned over, glass shattered, and the boy heard it. He looked out and recognized the intruder who, in turn, made a lunge for him. But Todd was too quick; he shut the door and locked it and made his call to 911. Finished with Wilma Danay, the killer couldn't leave the boy behind. He broke into the boy's room, but once again Todd was too quick for him. He got away."

"So the boy ran because he was frightened," Wyler recapitulated. "And the perp' chased him because he'd been recognized."

"Right."

"The original intent was to kill Wilma Danay for the inheritance."

"Right."

Both now looked to Norah for her reaction.

Norah shook her head. "Indications are that the intruder was well informed regarding Wilma Danay's doings. He knew she'd be playing bridge that Sunday night, and he must surely have known that Todd would be staying with her. So, if his purpose was to commit murder, he wouldn't have chosen a night when there was a possible witness present in the person of the boy."

"So we're back to kidnapping," Ferdi concluded.

"Right." Anxiety for Todd Millard's safety and then the assignment to the subway killings had caused Norah to neglect the customary routine of investigation. She had let things slip; she admitted it. Having secured her release for direct responsibility in the subway killings, she was confident she would solve the Danay case. But would she get Todd back.

Though she continued to insist he was still alive, in her heart a doubt was growing.

The provisions of the movie star's will offered a spring-board for the interrogation of those persons nearest to Wilma Danay. Of the three who had been with her on the fatal Sunday night, the one most obviously and openly in need of money was Nicholas Kouriades, the designer turned producer. However, he had an alibi, an alibi which now would be carefully scrutinized. Norah sent Simon, who had conducted the initial interview with Kouriades, to the neighborhood bar where Kouriades claimed to have stopped the Sunday night after the bridge game.

The next morning, armed with the information Simon elicited, Norah called on Kouriades.

It was just after nine and he was up and dressed. His eyes were clear and though his face sagged and his color was more a faded yellow than a glowing tan, there was no doubt he was a man with a purpose. A shadow passed over his face when he saw Norah Mulcahaney, but he smiled it away.

"Good morning, Lieutenant. Great morning, isn't it?"

In fact, it was. The sun shone in a clear blue sky, its light streaming through the high loft windows; the air was cool and crisp: a perfect fall day. Norah looked around, noting the architect's plans on the drawing board, the stack of manuscripts on the desk.

"Congratulations," she said.

Kouriades raised his eyebrows in question.

"I understand Miss Danay left you a considerable sum of money with which to produce your play."

"Thank you. Yes, that's true, she did. Dear Wilma."

"But I also heard that she didn't like the play. That she'd turned you down."

"No, no. It was certain production ideas she didn't like, but basically she was very high on the project. Otherwise, she wouldn't have left me the money, would she?"

"I suppose not."

"Of course not. So, what can I do for you, Lieutenant? I'm very busy. I'll be interviewing actors in a short while."

"I just have a couple of questions. It won't take long," she assured him as she pulled out a chair and sat down. "You did tell Detective Wyler that after the bridge game Sunday night you stopped in at the Golden Bear before coming home? You thought it was about ten-thirty."

"That's right."

"And you met a friend at the bar. The friend came back here with you and spent the night."

"All right, yes. I don't know what business it is of yours, but yes, it's true."

"When Detective Wyler was here Tuesday morning, you had a friend staying over," Norah remarked pleasantly. "The same one, I assume. That would be John Downing."

Kouriades's color faded some more.

Norah held up a hand. "Believe me, Mr. Kouriades, we have no wish to intrude into your private life, but if it was Mr. Downing, it struck Detective Wyler as odd that you didn't ask him to confirm your story right then. Of course, now we know it was because you hadn't had time to rehearse him."

"I don't know what you're talking about."

"There seems to be a difference of opinion about the time, Mr. Kouriades. A considerable difference. According to witnesses, you didn't get to the Golden Bear till close to midnight."

"What witnesses? Did you speak with my friend?"

"Downing? Yes. He was confused at first. But we helped clear his memory."

"What do you mean 'helped clear his memory'? What did you do to him?" Kouriades's color deepened to amber.

"We simply pointed out that the bartender at the Golden Bear was certain you didn't come in till midnight, and there were three other witnesses who agreed with him."

Sweat oozed out of the designer's coarse pores and his whole face glistened. "Why are you doing this to me?"

"Why did you lie the first time you were questioned? Why did you lie to Detective Wyler? Why did you prime your friend to support your lie?"

"Oh, God . . ." Slowly, the designer turned away and went over to the desk where, rummaging through the pile of papers, he found a pack of cigarettes. Empty. He threw it away with a shaking hand. "I lied because I knew that Detective Wyler and, ultimately, you, wouldn't believe the truth."

"Try me."

He fixed his dark eyes on Norah.

"I went back after the game to see Wilma. It was a rule that we shouldn't ever discuss business during bridge sessions, but I had to talk to her."

"The doorman doesn't remember your going back."

He shrugged. "I rode down with Pete and Cam Bouchard. Their car was in the garage, so they went all the way down to the basement. I got out at the lobby and took the next car back up. The elevators are out of the doorman's view."

"All right. Go on."

"The option I held on the play was about to run out. I wanted Wilma to lend me the money to renew, that was all. A couple of thousand would have done it."

"And did she agree?"

"Yes, she did." The question seemed to surprise him. "That is, she promised. She didn't have that much in the house, but she said she'd give it to me in the morning."

"Why didn't she just make out a check?"

"Wilma was very secretive about financial affairs. You learned not to ask too many questions."

In this case certainly convenient, Norah thought.

"Did you try to contact her on Monday morning?"

"No. The banks were closed. There wasn't any point."

"Ah . . ."

"She'd promised and she'd get around to it."

"Anyway, renewing the option was merely a stopgap, wasn't it?" Norah observed. "You needed a lot more than a couple of thousand to put the show on."

"I would have found it."

"But now you don't have to. I suggest that Wilma Danay did not promise to give you the money at all. She turned you down. She told you to stop bugging her or she'd cut you out of her will. You did know you were in the will, didn't you?"

He thought that one over too; Norah watched him. Once again he found a way to straddle.

"Sure, I knew. We all knew more or less. She told us herself. It was a way of keeping us in line. Rich people use the promise of money just as forcibly as the money itself."

"So she threatened to cut you out of the will and before she could do it, you killed her."

"No, no, I didn't; I swear I didn't." He found a handkerchief and mopped his face. "She promised to help me with the option money and she would have kept her promise. And she wouldn't have done that unless she intended to back me. She wouldn't have thrown good money away. Anyway, why pick on me? I'm not the only one who benefits from her death. Go talk to Pete and Cam; they're not as pure as they appear. Sure, Pete helped Wilma make a lot of money, but he didn't do so well for himself. Her death pulls some of his chestnuts out of the fire."

"What do you mean?"

Now Kouriades relaxed a little. "Go talk to Yolanda

Yates. Things between her and Wilma were far from perfect."

"But they were together so many years," Norah protested.

"Twenty-two," the designer provided promptly. "It isn't easy for two people, two women, to live together that long without some friction. Little irritants become major upsets. Affection can turn to dislike, or worse."

"Nevertheless, Yates is in the will," Norah told him. "Twenty-five thousand dollars may not be a lot of money nowadays and it isn't much compared to the other bequests, but she also had the promise of a comfortable subsistence for the rest of her life."

"And that's better than a kick in the pants, which is what she would have got after one more quarrel, one more disagreement," Kouriades insisted.

"How do you know?"

"Wilma told me. She groused about Yolanda continuously."

Chapter

FOURTEEN

Nick Kouriades was flailing out in all directions to turn attention from himself, but his allegations were certainly worth examining, Norah thought as she got into her car and headed uptown. Particularly intriguing was what he'd said about the Bouchards. Before approaching them a second time, however, she wanted to be sure that she was not dealing with gossip, or that Kouriades was not making the accusation out of malice. She decided to assign Danny Neel and Julius Ochs to inquire into the Bouchards' financial position.

But what most intrigued Norah was Wilma Danay's treatment of her daughter. The will was drawn up in such a way that Adele could not get her hands on the capital. Wilma Danay had in essence disinherited her daughter. Why? Was it her daughter's financial judgment she didn't trust? Was she afraid Adele would use the money carelessly or be drawn into bad investments? Or did she think Adele would squander the money in high living? She didn't seem the type.

Through the period she'd been occupied with the subway case, Norah had nevertheless kept in touch with Mrs. Millard, calling at least once a day. It was not satisfactory for either one of them. Norah decided she needed to speak with

Adele Millard in person. They had never really talked. Norah didn't really know her, but having herself lost a child she felt a strong sympathy toward her. Adele Millard was still living in her mother's apartment, still waiting. In the past when Norah called it was she who picked up the phone and never later than the second ring. This time the phone was answered late and by the companion.

"Mrs. Millard is out. She won't be back till three."

"I'll stop by then."

Instead of sending out for her usual tuna on toast and coffee, Norah decided to treat herself to a real lunch in a restaurant. Today, after all, was her birthday. The dreaded fortieth had finally arrived.

She didn't feel any different, Norah thought. She'd insisted to all who had put out feelers that she didn't want any fuss, and so far that wish had been respected. She had gotten brief salutations from each man in the squad room when she came in. There had been cards in the mail from the family. Signora Emilia, Joe's mother, had wanted to make a family dinner; with all of Joe's seven sisters and their husbands and children; it would have been more than Norah could have coped with. She told her mother-in-law honestly that she wasn't in the mood for celebrations. Signora Emilia understood. So the phone wouldn't be ringing at home tonight, Norah thought. It was and would be a day like any other. The way she wanted. Why should she feel disappointed?

But she could go out for lunch. She chose a new Italian restaurant around the corner from the station house. It was small and, probably because it was yet to be discovered, quiet. She ate in leisurely fashion and by the time she was finished with a very good fettucine Alfredo, even after lingering over the cappuccino, it was still too early to meet Mrs. Millard but too late for it to be worthwhile to go back to the office. She decided on a stroll in the park. She took the lake path, her favorite. It was far enough inside so that sound from the street didn't intrude, and at this hour with the children in school and most people at work, she had it to herself. There was little wind, and the November sun was warm. The water lapped gently at the shore. An occasional squirrel scampered through the blanket of dry leaves, golden and russett. This place had many memories for Norah. Crimes had been committed here that she investigated. On other occasions, she had come carrying personal burdens and found surcease.

She didn't realize how much time had passed till she felt the chill of the shadows as the sun sank in the sky behind the Gulf and Western Building. She looked at her watch; nearly three. She'd have to hurry.

She reached the Danay apartment just after three. Yolanda Yates admitted her and ushered her to the salon where Adele Millard was waiting.

"Is there news?"

There was both hope and dread in the question. She should have realized, Norah thought, that Mrs. Millard would assume her request for a meeting meant there was a new development. "No, nothing. I'm sorry."

"At least it's not bad news." Her disappointment was obvious.

"I assume you haven't been contacted?"

"No, I don't believe I'll ever hear from him again."

At that, Yolanda Yates made a little whimpering sound of compassion, but a frown from Mrs. Millard silenced her. Mrs. Millard picked up a leather briefcase from the sofa.

"I'm sorry I can't talk to you further, Lieutenant. I'm due at a meeting." She glanced at her watch. "In fact, overdue."

She was dressed in another of her severely tailored suits, this one of dark gray twill with a short skirt that showed off her legs and a rose-colored blouse that was kind to her

161

complexion. She looked, all in all, more composed than the last and only time Norah had seen her, but still under considerable strain.

"Life goes on, Lieutenant. It has to."

"Yes," Norah said. "I do need to speak to you."

"Of course, if you don't mind calling my secretary for a time. I have no idea what my schedule is like."

And she was gone.

"I hope this isn't a bad time for *you*, Miss Yates?" Norah asked the companion.

"I'm expecting the appraiser. Everything has to be appraised for tax purposes," she explained. "But he's not due for another hour."

"I won't keep you that long."

Restored to order, the size and elegance of the entrance gallery and the salon could be appreciated. There were three seating areas, the principal one arranged around the fireplace and focusing on a life-size oil portrait of the star over the mantel. Yolanda Yates was about to sit in a bergère-style chair beneath it, but at the last moment she changed her mind and chose instead a settee on the far side of the room.

Norah joined her. The companion, too, had undergone a change in the past couple of weeks. She looked more rested, more at ease. She wore a pale blue silk dress with a full skirt and flowing sleeves that softened her angular frame. Unfortunately, she spoiled the effect with ropes of fake pearls, and her blonde hair remained dry and overbleached.

"Is Mrs. Millard still living here or has she gone back to her own place?" Norah wanted to know.

"She's still here. How much longer she intends to stay, I have no idea. She wanted to be available as long as there was a chance of hearing from the kidnapper, but, as you know, she's given up."

"How about you? Do you think there's still a possibility the kidnapper will make contact?"

"I don't know."

Norah looked long and thoughtfully at the woman. "I have to ask you some personal questions, Miss Yates. I hope you won't be offended and will answer. It's important to the investigation."

"I'll do my best."

Norah nodded. "It's in regard to Miss Danay's will. After a lifetime's relationship, aren't you disappointed, even hurt, by your treatment? The money seems a token sum for all your years of devotion. The living provisions look like charity."

The woman was embarrassed. "I don't think you have the right to ask that."

"I'm exploring motive, Miss Yates."

"Motive? For what? For kidnapping Todd? That's obvious. Money. But I . . ."

"For the murder of Wilma Danay."

"Murder? I thought . . . I don't understand."

"Certain evidence leads us to believe the motive behind the break-in Sunday night might not have been to snatch the boy but to kill Miss Danay." Norah watched Yates carefully. Would she buy it?

It took a while for the companion to digest that. "And you think I did it? I wasn't even here, for God's sake! You know that. You know I was on the train from Montreal. You talked to my sister. You were right here when I got back from my trip."

"A trip made in response to an accident that never happened."

"That's right. It was a mistake. By the hospital. One of those things. The point is I couldn't be in two places at the same time."

"And you feel no resentment toward Miss Danay?"

"Resentment? No, certainly not. You only know part of the story, Lieutenant. Wilma was not easy to live with, I grant you. But she made up for her tantrums with great generosity. She promised me that I would always have a place to live and that I would be cared for. And that she fulfilled. As for the money, she didn't have to leave me anything. When I first came to work for her, while she was still active in pictures, I was in love with a young man, very handsome but not very honest. He was always borrowing money from me for schemes that never panned out. When I had no more money to give, because he never paid anything back, he wanted me to go to Miss Danay. I couldn't do that. Anyway, I didn't think she'd give it to me. To get to the point, Lance talked me into passing some of her jewels to him so that he could have copies made. I put the copies back and he hocked the originals to pay his gambling debts. He promised to return the originals before she could ever find out.

"Well, you know what happened, Lieutenant. Once he had the jewels, I never saw him again."

"What was the young man's name?"

"Henry Lancelot."

"I assume Miss Danay did ultimately find out."

Yolanda Yates sighed heavily. "I had to tell her. The jewels were never recovered and there was no way I could pay back their value, but she forgave me. She kept me on. And she never, in all the years, threw it up to me. And now she's provided for me for the rest of my life. How can I feel anything but gratitude?"

Norah nodded. "And how does Mrs. Millard feel about the will? She's as much as disinherited."

"That's not true."

"She's limited to an allowance and that in turn is subject to the discretion of an executor, Peter Bouchard, and later on when her son reaches the age of eighteen she'll be dependent on him. At the least, it's a humiliation."

"No, on the contrary, it's more than Adele expected.

Adele has already received her inheritance. Her mother gave her one million dollars to buy into the firm of Hammer, Prescott."

Norah was impressed. A company might be a giant in its field and not be known by the general public. Hammer, Prescott was small, but the name evoked instant recognition.

"The bequest provides a cushion in case the business goes bad, which Wilma feared. It shows how much her mother really cared for Adele despite all their differences."

"Such as?"

"Adele married young and she married a much older man. Wilma didn't approve."

"She did the same thing herself, didn't she?" Norah pointed out. "Frank Grillo, Adele's father, was twenty years older than Wilma."

"Exactly, and it didn't work out. Wilma argued the whole age disparity problem. She also delved into the cultural difference between Adele and Richard, but Adele wouldn't listen. She was in love. Somehow, Wilma forgot about that; she forgot what a woman will do when she's in love." She paused.

Remembering what she had done? Norah wondered.

"Anyway, Adele eloped and then presented her mother with the accomplished fact. Unless she wanted to lose her daughter, Wilma had no choice but to accept Richard. When Todd was born, Wilma made a complete about-face. She became the doting grandmother. Everything was judged on the basis of the boy's welfare.

"Meantime, the marriage wasn't going well. Adele felt unfulfilled and wanted out. As much as she'd been opposed to the marriage, Wilma now fought the divorce. According to her, Adele had made her bed and she should lie in it."

"There's no mention of Richard Millard in the will except in the eventuality of Adele's death," Norah recalled.

"That's right. Wilma blamed him for the divorce. She contended that he didn't recognize his wife's need to be an individual. For all his avowed liberalism, he wanted to limit her activities to the home. Presumably his new wife is satisfied with that kind of life. And I suppose Richard is content to fulfill his role as breadwinner without the monetary assistance Adele received from Wilma."

So according to Yolanda Yates everyone was provided for and content.

"How's the advertising business these days?" Norah asked.

"Good," the companion replied. "As far as I know. Adele doesn't talk about it."

Norah put out another feeler. "I've heard rumors that Peter Bouchard is not doing so well financially."

"I wouldn't know about that."

"Miss Danay didn't mention it?"

"No. I don't think she would have kept Pete Bouchard as executor if she had any doubts about his judgment. Who told you he was in trouble?"

"I can't say."

"Well, if you got it from Nicky Kouriades, I'd advise you not to put too much stock in it. Nicky has it in for Pete because Pete advised Wilma against investing in his new show."

"Advice which, in the end, she didn't follow."

Yolanda Yates looked to the portrait of the famous actress. "She liked to play them one against the other."

Norah looked up, too, and it seemed that Wilma Danay returned the look. "One last question, Miss Yates. What do you think happened to Todd Millard? Is he still alive?"

A shudder passed through the woman. She clasped her hands in her lap tightly but couldn't stop them shaking. A nerve twitched under her left eye. "I don't know what happened. I don't know. But I believe he's still alive. I believe it!"

It was, Norah thought, her first honest and spontaneous reaction.

It wasn't easy for Detectives Neel and Ochs to track down the information regarding the financial status of the Bouchards that Norah needed. It took several days, but it was worth waiting for, and she went to her second interview with them well prepared.

As before, she was received graciously. The hour, five in the afternoon, was comfortable for them as actors; the peak period of activity was drawing near. Outside, dusk was deepening into night and the theater marquees were lit and, although they were not themselves performing, the excitement coursed through their blood. Inside the elegant apartment, the lights glowed, softening the austerity of the modern decor and enhancing the colors of the paintings individually and as a collection. The first time Norah had been there she hadn't examined them closely. She did so now while waiting for the famous couple to make an entrance. She proceeded from one canvas to the next, studying each, taking her time. Though she heard their steps behind her, Norah continued till she'd seen them all.

"You have quite a collection," she observed, having completed the full tour of the room. "It must have taken you many years."

"A lifetime."

"Every one is beautiful."

"Thank you."

Balancing himself on a pair of canes, Peter Bouchard made his way to his special oversized and reenforced chair and lowered himself into it. With the rolls of his belly overlapping his belt, jowls sagging, eyes sleepy slits, he was more Buddhalike than ever. Camilla Bouchard, on the other hand, appeared to have shed years. She looked like a pixie. Had she ever played Peter Pan? Norah wondered.

"Of course, I'm no expert," Norah said. "I can't tell which are authentic and which are copies."

It was a bombshell and it left both the Bouchards momentarily stunned. Peter Bouchard gasped for breath, his enormous chest heaving. It took several moments before his wife could shake off the shock and go to him.

With a wave he indicated he was all right. "You're joking, of course, Lieutenant," he managed finally to speak. "But it's in very poor taste."

"I'm not joking," she assured him. From her large handbag Norah pulled a sheaf of papers. "This is a partial list of what you've sold and to whom. My people are tracing the rest. According to what we have so far, you started divesting yourself of art works, paintings, and sculptures, right after the crash of eighty-seven. You were heavily into the market and on margin to the extent the law allowed at that time. On the Tuesday after Black Monday, your broker called on you to cover your position. You had no option but to sell off some of your treasures. I can imagine it wasn't easy."

She waited, but so did they.

"According to our information, the first item to go was the Degas." Norah went over and stood in front of the painting, which depicted a ballerina in the traditional frothy white tutu bending down in the classic pose to wind the pale pink ribbons of her dancing slippers. "It was acquired by Horace Templeton, a collector as well known as yourself, reportedly for two and a quarter million. You would have got more if you'd put it up for auction, but you didn't want anybody to know you were selling, particularly Wilma Danay. Anyway, you did sell it, yet here it is hanging on your wall."

She paused. "Question: which is the authentic Degas, his or yours?"

Still, Bouchard didn't speak.

"You managed to survive, but apparently you didn't learn anything from the experience. Trying to recoup your losses, you jumped back into the market. You turned gambler instead of investor. You bought *puts,* sold short, even shorted the Dow Jones, which I'm told is a very risky business, indeed, even for the experts. And you got burned again! Wilma Danay, on the other hand, didn't follow your lead. You had been her financial guide over the years with good success, but this time she had a hunch, or a premonition, if you prefer. At least, that's what she told her broker when she ordered him to sell all her holdings. She got out of the market in July of eighty-seven, well before the crash, and she stayed out. Did she know how hard you were hit?"

Bouchard cleared his throat. "Will you get me my medication, Camilla, please?" He asked and waited till his wife had left the room. "No. I let her think I got out at about the same time she did."

"Why?" Norah knew the answer but she wanted him to say it.

"Because she would have needled me about it. She would never have let me forget that she had been smarter than me. She would never have let up."

"And . . .?"

"And what?"

"She would have removed you as executor of her estate."

"No, of course not. One had nothing to do with the other."

"She would have lost faith in your judgment. She wouldn't have trusted you to administer, conserve, and increase what she had left for her grandson."

"All right, she might have. Probably, she would have," he admitted. "Then, later on, she would have reinstated me. It's a thankless job anyway, an obligation. To tell you the truth, I'm not particularly looking forward to it."

"It's a job that puts you in control of twelve million dollars."

"It's a heavy responsibility."

"The first time around, in eighty-seven, you took a bath, as they say on the Street, but you had assets you could convert." Norah indicated the paintings. "You were able to cover your losses and start trading again. For a while you were doing all right, then the market took another plunge. But this time you had nothing to fall back on, nothing left to sell. No use asking Wilma Danay for a loan, you knew that. Close as you were, she wouldn't have given you any money; she had no respect for losers, or pity. But if she died, you'd get what she'd left you in her will—the paintings and also the jewels she'd bequeathed to your wife. In addition, you'd have control of the entire estate."

"You can't be serious, Lieutenant!" Camilla Bouchard exclaimed in her light, airy voice. She came forward carrying a glass of water and two pills on a small silver salver along with a dainty napkin, which she proffered to her husband.

"If we were so broke, how was Peter able to raise two hundred and fifty thousand dollars for Todd's ransom in a matter of hours? How did he manage that, Lieutenant?"

"Adele Millard offered to sell you her mother's Bonnard," Norah replied to Camilla's question but addressed herself to her husband. "You had no money to buy it, but you knew someone who did and who could also raise a large part of the price in cash very quickly. Someone with whom you'd done business before. Your fellow collector, Horace Templeton. So you sold the Bonnard to him for two hundred and fifty thousand in advance against a total of one million."

"No," Bouchard grunted. "Absolutely not."

"You would give another two hundred and fifty thousand

to Mrs. Millard as agreed and come out of it with five hundred thousand for yourself. Not a bad deal."

"All right. So I made a profit on a quick turnover. What's wrong with that?"

"Nothing," Norah replied. "I'm only interested in the transaction as it's indicative of your financial situation. Mr. Templeton was reluctant to admit anything; that was part of his arrangement with you. But once we convinced him that he had done nothing wrong and would only be in trouble if he withheld evidence, he confirmed the whole story. We have his signed deposition."

It was as though Norah had stuck a pin into a balloon; the actor's defiance gushed out and the huge bulk of flabby flesh deflated. His wife, standing beside him, took up the defense.

"All right, so we had bad luck in the market. So we sold our paintings. They were ours to sell. We hung copies in our own living room in our own home. We didn't do anything wrong. That's not against the law. And we're far from broke. We still have this apartment, for instance. You can't seriously accuse my husband of being responsible for what happened to Wilma! Of breaking into her apartment, trashing the place, beating her up, knocking her around? Look at him. For God's sake, Lieutenant, look at him! He can hardly get out of that chair unassisted. He can't make it across the room without his canes. Besides, I can swear he was here at home when it happened. We left Wilma's shortly after ten and came straight home. And stayed home, both of us. We watched the eleven o'clock news and went to bed."

She thrust the salver at her husband. "Take your pills, Peter."

He had trouble swallowing. Some of the water trickled down his chin.

"I'll ask you to leave now, Lieutenant. You've done enough damage." Using the dainty napkin, she cleaned him up.

Chapter

FIFTEEN

David Juvelis was waiting in her office when Norah returned. She hadn't spoken to him since the failed stakeout, and from the look of him he hadn't come to bring good news. They shook hands; she waved him to a seat.

"So?"

"You haven't been around lately."

"I've been working on the Danay case."

He nodded. "We're going to do another stakeout."

"Might as well."

He frowned. "But you don't think so?"

"Unless we have some idea who the perp' is or what he looks like, we're spinning our wheels."

"We've talked to every patient Thelma Harrison ever attended both in the hospital and privately in the patient's home. Nothing. I think it's time to move on to Joanna Christie."

Norah realized he was asking for her opinion and she was pleased. "It doesn't make sense for the second victim to be the key. Unless . . . Are we missing something?"

"What?"

"How do we know Thelma Harrison was the first?"

Juvelis shrugged.

"She went off the platform on October fifteenth. Were

there any incidents prior to that date? Christie was killed on November twelfth and Helen Wyatt on the nineteenth. That was when a pattern was discerned." It was, in fact, the media who designated Thelma Harrison as the first victim and started counting, Norah thought. "I think we should consider the possibility that there was at least one other victim prior to Thelma."

"You mean check out the fatalities over the whole system?" Clearly, the prospect was daunting.

"It's not necessary," Norah reassured him. "These three young women went off the same platform. That's what first attracted our attention, drew us to recognize a pattern. All you need now is to check the records of that one station. It shouldn't take long. It should punch right up on the computer."

Norah got the call two hours later. The excitement was in Juvelis's voice.

"We've got something. I'm not exactly sure how it fits, but it has to fit."

"What? Why aren't you sure?" Norah was excited, too.

"There was an earlier death on the tracks at the lower level of that same station one year prior to Harrison's. It happened October sixteenth, also a Monday."

"What's the problem?"

"The victim was eighty-two years old."

"Ah . . ."

"Her name is Hester Gorin and she suffered from Alzheimer's. She was under home care attended by a visiting RN. On this particular day, she managed to give the nurse the slip. That Monday was not the first time Mrs. Gorin had got out on her own, but it was her last. Witnesses on the platform at the time stated she waved as though to stop the train and then jumped in front of it."

"Suicide?"

"They said it was like she was trying to hail a cab or stop a bus. I suppose you could call it accidental suicide, if there is such a thing."

"And who was the RN?" Norah asked and held her breath.

"Thelma Harrison."

She expelled it. "Wasn't the name Gorin on the list of Harrison's patients?"

"It was," Juvelis replied. "She left a son, Nathaniel."

"I assume he was interviewed."

"Sure, along with two hundred and forty-two patients, their relatives, friends, and enemies."

"How about when his mother died?" Norah asked.

"Yeah. Right. According to the report, Gorin was at work when it happened. He got a frantic call from Harrison telling him his mother had got away, wandered off, and she had no idea where. He called 911 though Harrison told him she'd already done that. Then he went to the station house, which at that time was temporarily on Ninety-sixth. By the time he got there the body on the tracks had been identified and a cop was waiting to escort him down to the morgue. He blamed Harrison. His mother had been in her care. For a while it looked like she might be charged with negligence, but after the testimony of Mrs. Gorin's physician and her neighbors in the apartment building as to the elderly woman's mental stability, or instability, Thelma Harrison was exonerated."

"How about the second canvass? What did he have to say then?"

"Gorin acknowledged that Thelma Harrison had taken care of his mother. She would come in at seven A.M. just as he was going to work. Her job was to dress and feed the patient, give her medication, and *watch her*. Gorin admitted that his mother had a habit of wandering away. At the end of the day, the nurse gave Mrs. Gorin her evening meal and put her to bed. He came home from work and took over. The idea was never to leave her alone. Harrison was competent, even dedicated, Gorin said, but as the illness progressed, his mother became more and more difficult to handle. The strain was telling on him. She had tantrums, turned violent so that he had to restrain her. He had no choice but to place her in a nursing home and let Harrison go."

"This is the story he's telling now?"

"Right."

"Did anybody check the nursing home?"

Juvelis groaned. "At the time we had no reason to doubt him. He appeared absolutely forthcoming. If you hadn't suggested looking up previous fatalities from that station . . ."

"What did you find out?"

"No Hester Gorin is listed as ever having been a patient."

"So he lied," Norah said.

"Oh, we'll break him down. I'll handle the interrogation myself."

"I don't know. Say you do break him down and he admits he lied the second time around, what good will it do us?"

"We'll know why he lied."

"We already know, don't we?"

"We know that he blamed Thelma Harrison for the death of his mother. Our investigation exonerated her. He went over our heads to NYPD and got nowhere. So he took justice into his own hands."

"Right."

"But why the others? They were innocent women who had nothing to do with his mother," Juvelis exclaimed.

"We both know the answer to that," Norah replied. "He's symbolically killing Harrison over and over again. He waited a year nurturing the need for vengeance. He kept watch over Harrison, and it must have seemed the hand of Providence that she regularly used the same subway station and stood on the same platform from which his mother had jumped. Finally as the anniversary of her death drew near, he couldn't contain himself. He followed the nurse and shoved her into the path of the oncoming train so that she died in the same way his mother had.

"That brought relief, but not for long," Norah went on. "Vengeance had been the focus of his life for a year and he was empty without it. He started haunting the subway station again. He found someone similar in age and appearance to Harrison and killed again. There was another period of relief, but shorter. Each time he killed, the need became greater. I'm told that's classic in cases of this kind.

"Up to now, not a shadow of suspicion had touched him. He felt completely safe. If you go back and take another turn at interrogating him, he'll know he's threatened. Then what will he do? How will he react?"

"Maybe he'll stop," Juvelis suggested.

"It's possible. I wish he would, but I don't think so. He waited a year to commit his first murder. It was only a month after that he shoved Joanna Christie over the edge to her death. One week later he went after Helen Wyatt. He's developing a taste for it."

"A compulsion," Juvelis suggested.

"Yes." Norah agreed. "When his mother died he appealed to the authorities for justice. He didn't get it, not according to his lights, so he took matters into his own hands. Maybe he didn't expect to be interrogated when Harrison died. Maybe he didn't think we'd make the connection, so he panicked and lied. If you go back once more there's no way you can pass it off as routine. He'll know for sure you've discovered his lie. He'll know he's in danger and he may change his m.o or his timetable. Then we won't have any lead to him at all."

"Okay. So we play it straight. We charge him with homicide, put him under severe interrogation, and get a confession."

"Which he later retracts, and charges police brutality."

"That's for the lawyers. It's not our problem."

"It is in my book, David." It was the first time Norah had used his first name. "At best, we're developing a case based on circumstantial evidence. We ought at least to make it a strong one."

"Right."

"For now, let him think we buy his story. On the qt, we start checking out Mr. Gorin's alibis for each of the three killings; we find out where he was and what he was doing and with whom."

"How about this coming Monday? Suppose he shows up on the platform ready to do his number?"

"You said the brass wants another stakeout. We know who he is, where he lives, what he looks like. This time we've got a big jump on him."

Again Norah had to set aside her work on the Danay case. As she studied the subway killer's profile as drawn by the police psychiatrist, his Behavioral Profile, Norah was impressed by how well the facts turned by David's interrogation fit. Even the photograph taken from a distance with a Telephoto lens was right. It showed a man in his late thirties, well-built, pale-complexioned, with mild, blue-gray eyes. He was almost handsome in a low-key way. Certainly, he didn't look dangerous or threatening. If he walked up to a woman, she would have no reason to draw back, Norah thought, not at first anyway. By the time she became aware of danger, it would be too late.

In consultation, the brass of both forces agreed to call on a SWAT team and stake out the lower level of the station. It was not deemed necessary to turn out large numbers; this time they had a tail on the suspect. Norah had assigned her three top people—Arenas, Wyler, and Neel—to be partnered by their opposite numbers on the Transit force to keep Gorin under surveillance around the clock. Large numbers at the station were not only unnecessary but increased the risk the suspect might make them and the operation would fail once again.

Positions were taken at four o'clock. Looking over the arrangements, Norah could find nothing wrong, yet she was nervous. Having spotted the cops, she now swept the platform for likely victims. Two women stepped off the escalator—each one fulfilled the requirements as to age and looks and both got on trains and were gone in minutes. There was no sign of Gorin. Contact by two-way radio with the surveillance team had been ruled out for fear Gorin might catch on.

By six-thirty, the rush hour was over. The number of passengers had lessened and conditions for the killer were no longer optimum. The stakeout was called off. Norah and Juvelis went their separate ways: Norah, back to the squad, and David, home or to his girlfriend; she supposed he had a girlfriend. She knew very little about David Juvelis, Norah thought; she hadn't had the time or, to be honest, the curiosity to find out. He was a good officer, dedicated, intelligent, smart enough to know he was still learning. If they managed to catch this killer, it would be in large part due to David Juvelis's work. In the past Norah had not been enthusiastic about the concept of merging the two departments. Because of David she was having second thoughts.

Her phone was ringing. She picked it up right away, not even pausing to pull out her chair and sit.

"Homicide, Fourth Division. Mulcahaney."

"Lieutenant . . ."

"Simon! What's happened?" She knew right away it wasn't going to be good news.

"We lost him."

She caught her breath. After a moment, she asked, "How?"

"He came out of the electronics store where he works and headed uptown. He usually walks home and we fell in behind. A bus stopped at a corner and blocked our view for a few moments. When it pulled out, we saw that he was on it."

"You think he made you?" she asked.

"Honestly, no, Lieutenant. I don't see how he could."

If he'd made a mistake, Wyler would admit it, Norah thought. She couldn't imagine him being so clumsy. His Transit partner she couldn't vouch for, but Simon wouldn't put the blame on him even if he deserved it.

"Where are you now?"

"Around the corner from his apartment on Seventieth."

"I'll send someone to relieve you, then you come on in." She hung up.

Wyler and his partner were off the case, obviously, but should the surveillance be continued or had it been blown? If Gorin knew he was being tailed, the situation was bad, very bad. Couldn't be much worse.

She was wrong. She found out how wrong when the phone rang an hour later.

"Fourth, Homicide. Mulcahaney."

"He's done it again. At the Sixty-eighth Street station."

No need to ask who it was; she recognized David's voice. The background noise consisted of many voices and their hollow echoes. He must be at the scene. The power would have been shut off and the trains would not be running.

"When?" she asked.

"Right after we called the watch off at Sixtieth."

"Are you sure this is him, not a copycat?"

"Except for the place everything else is the same: the day and the time; well, maybe a half hour later than the others. The victim is female, Caucasian, medium height and build, dark, curly hair, about twenty-two years old. Student at Hunter College. Name of Sabrina Brownwell."

"Should I come over?"

"If you want, but we have things in hand. We're questioning witnesses."

"You've got witnesses?"

"Giving the usual conflicting reports: the perp' was hustling the victim for a handout; the perp' wasn't anywhere near her till he jumped her. She was talking to him; she had her back to him. He was tall; he was short; he was bent over so that you couldn't tell. Nobody even tried to guess his age. There was agreement on only one thing: he was one of the homeless."

"Could it have been a disguise?"

"I'll bet the farm on it," Juvelis answered. "We didn't avenge his mother's death, so he took justice into his own hands. Now he's challenging us to catch him." He paused. "We've got to pick Gorin up. We have no choice."

"Right. Only—he may not be sitting in his apartment waiting for us. It's possible he made the tail."

Juvelis's comment was a long, low whistle. "There's only one way to find out. Should we go together?"

It was supposed to be a joint venture, but the case belonged to David and had from the beginning, Norah thought. If there was going to be a bust, he should get the credit. "Would you mind if I passed? I've got a hunch I'm close to a break on the Danay case."

"Sure. I understand. Good luck." He hesitated. "Thanks, Norah."

* * *

What Norah had told David Juvelis was true; she did feel she was on the verge of solving Wilma Danay's murder. The answer lay in the maze of emotional relationships she had so far explored. She was looking at it and didn't recognize it. So she did what Joe had taught her to do—she collected all of the pertinent material and took it home with her to review: every report, every interview, every notation including her own, over and over again and then again. Certain refinements had been added over the years. First, a relaxing hot bath. Then she got into pajamas and robe. Had a light snack, soup or a peanut butter sandwich. Then, finally, she got to work.

By one A.M., Norah had gone over everything twice and decided she should give her subconscious a chance. As she got up to stretch, the telephone rang. It startled her. She decided to let the answering machine kick in.

"Norah, this is David." He sounded tired and discouraged. "He hasn't shown up. I think he's skipped."

She raced for the receiver, picked it up, and pushed the stop button on the machine. "Are you sure?"

"No, I can't be, not without entering the apartment to see what he's taken, if anything. I don't think that's a good idea."

"No, I agree." So Gorin *had* made the tail, she thought. Smart as he was, probably he'd been looking for it. Damn. What was really bad was not just that Gorin knew they had identified him as the perp', but that he was no longer limiting himself to the one subway station on his prowl for victims. True, he had moved only one stop away, but having moved once, he could do it again. And probably would. He might strike anywhere in the system.

"So what are you going to do?" Norah asked Juvelis.

"Wait. What else?"

And the city would wait with him, Norah thought, and hold its breath.

Her concentration broken, Norah decided she might as well call it a night and go to bed. She slept soundly and woke before her alarm went off, feeling surprisingly optimistic. God knew why, she thought, listening to the radio as she got dressed. The death of yet another young woman on the tracks, Sabrina Brownwell, was the lead story. As Norah had feared, the media took it as established that the city was afflicted by a serial killer whose attacks were no longer restricted to one platform of one station, but could occur anywhere underground. Every kind of citizens' committee demanded action. The mayor, the police commissioner, the Transit police chief, all were trying to quell the storm. They were interviewed and gave statements; they sounded ineffectual. The investigation was making *good headway,* they said. They had a *strong lead. An arrest was imminent,* the mayor assured them. Under the battery of questions that statement set off, he cringed. *He couldn't say more for fear of compromising the case.*

He shouldn't have said that much, Norah thought.

Her phone rang. She had a pretty good idea what it would be about and she wasn't wrong. She was being summoned to the office of the C of D in the big building. *Forthwith,* of course. She gulped a cup of coffee, skipped her regular breakfast, and decided the subway would be faster than driving. As it happened, the station nearest Norah's apartment was the one where the latest victim had met her death. It served Hunter College and was heavily used, though it seemed somewhat less busy this morning. Looking around, Norah could find no indication of yesterday's tragedy. At the roar of an oncoming train, she hastily drew back from the edge of the platform. She noticed everyone else did the same.

She was glad she was being summoned by Chief Deland rather than by his opposite number at Transit, Charles Aspen. She was not surprised, however, when she entered Deland's waiting room to find David Juvelis already there. He gave her a nervous grin but didn't say anything. She wanted to offer some word of encouragement but decided it might make him even more nervous. So they sat in silence for about fifteen minutes before the door of the chief's private office opened and David was waved inside. Norah got up at the same time, but Vivian Kamenan, the chief's civilian secretary, indicated it wasn't her turn.

Norah didn't like that they were being seen separately. Were they trying to fix the blame for the failed surveillance? Another fifteen minutes passed with agonizing slowness and finally David emerged. He was pale, dazed. And relieved? She wasn't sure. But she got the signal to go in and couldn't talk to him.

Chief Deland sat at his desk with Bureau Chief Jim Felix at his right. Transit Chief of Police Ben Woitach and his top man, Charles Aspen, were at the left. Their looks suggested to Norah that they'd already come to a conclusion, that policy had been determined, whether before or after David's input she had no way of knowing. Certainly before hers, she thought as she took the chair Chief Deland indicated.

He made the introductions and then got right to it.

"What happened yesterday, Lieutenant?"

"I don't know, Chief," she answered promptly. "We had the station covered: entrances and exits at both ends, upper and lower platforms, though all previous incidents had taken place at the lower. He didn't show."

"He went to another station instead."

"It looks that way."

"So he knew that a trap had been set."

Is that what David told them, that the suspect had made

Wyler and his partner? All right, so now was the time to give them a little background, Norah decided. "We conducted a routine check of previous victims at the Fifty-ninth Street station going back as far as we could and discovered that an elderly woman, Hester Gorin, suffering from Alzheimer's, escaped her nurse and either fell or jumped to the tracks from that platform over a year ago. The nurse was Thelma Harrison." Norah paused. She chose her next words carefully. "I'm convinced Mrs. Gorin's death is the link between all these subsequent murders."

No one commented, so Norah went on. "Her son, Nathaniel Gorin, blamed his mother's death on Thelma Harrison's negligence. He wanted to bring charges against her, but the police investigation exonerated her and he had to drop them. This time around, when he was interrogated regarding Harrison's death, he admitted that she had taken care of his mother, but he claimed his mother's condition got so bad at the end that he had to put her in a nursing home. He asserted that at the time of her death, Mrs. Gorin was no longer in Harrison's charge. We checked the nursing home and they'd never had a patient by that name. We decided not to challenge him on it or to confront him with his earlier testimony and his accusations against Harrison. We didn't want him to feel threatened. But," Norah sighed, "he's been under a lot of stress going back to his mother's death and before that during her illness. He's thirty-nine years old and has lived with her every one of those years. As far as we know, he's had no other female relationships. His mother's protracted illness was a drain; her death and the manner of it, traumatic. For over a year he's brooded. He would have been very sensitive to an atmosphere of danger."

"Why didn't you pick him up?"

Again she wondered what David had said. "I felt we lacked the evidence to make the charge stick, sir. We did put a tail on him."

"Which he lost," Deland pointed out.

"Yes, sir." So David had told them. "I'd like to say one thing for the record." Norah looked first to Deland and Felix, then to the two Transit officers. "As soon as we made the connection between Thelma Harrison and Nathaniel Gorin, Detective Juvelis wanted to go right over and get him. I was the one who ruled it out."

Deland nodded. "Thank you, Lieutenant."

Charles Aspen was not soothed. "You left him free to shove another innocent woman under a train."

"If it was a copy-cat crime, and I believe it was, then it would have happened anyway," Norah reasoned. "The scene was different, and that suggests . . ."

Benjamin Woitach cut her short. "I don't think we want to open that can of worms, Lieutenant."

Norah understood. It was bad enough to have one psycho haunting one location, but precautions could be taken: the number of cops patroling the area increased around the clock if necessary, and the public undoubtedly would stay away from that particular location. Once the *me too's* came out of their holes and the public learned there could be more than one obsessed killer roaming the system, control of any kind would become impossible.

Norah raised her chin; her blue eyes flashed directly at the Transit chief. "We daren't *not* open it, sir."

Deland was quick to take charge again before it turned into a confrontation. A sharp look warned Norah of her place and another look reminded Woitach that this officer was under his, Deland's, command.

"Your analysis makes sense, Lieutenant. You've identified the perpetrator; now it's up to the rest of us to find and apprehend him. Gorin's apartment is already staked out. We'll flood the city with his photo. It will be published on the front page of every newspaper and blown up on every newscast. We'll put out an APB. Let him know he's a wanted man. Let him know that he could be recognized at any moment by any citizen. The time for subtlety is past."

"Excuse me, sir." Norah had been waiting for a chance to speak.

"What, Lieutenant?"

She cast a look at Felix. "Despite the varied descriptions, all the witnesses agree it was a homeless person who committed the crime. I suggest he was disguised."

"Yes." Woitach looked hard at her. "Of course. Good point, Lieutenant. All right, we'll have the artist touch up the photo. Chief Aspen and Chief Felix will mount the search."

She hadn't expected anything else. She was, in fact, relieved.

"If we throw out the net and don't bring him in, then we'll have to take more direct and aggressive action," Deland continued. "According to the profile developed by the FBI's Behavioral Science Unit, the need to avenge his mother was frustrated yesterday because he was not able to push the victim . . ." He held up a hand to forestall Norah. ". . . off the same platform where his mother had met her death. For practical purposes we're assuming that was the killer and not a copycat. All right, Lieutenant?"

Norah bowed her head. Chief Deland was getting charged up, always a good sign.

"At this moment the killer is both frustrated and stimulated. He needs to take action, but the psychiatrists feel he will wait till Monday. I hope by then we will have apprehended him. If not . . ." Deland frowned, making it apparent to Norah anyway that the alternative was not to his liking. "If not, we'll have to go underground one more time."

Whereas Chief Aspen was very much in favor. "We have decided to lure him with a decoy. Up to now he's controlled us. We were in a position where we could only react. He selected the victim. We had to guess who it would be. We didn't know either him or the victim. This time we're going to know both. It'll be our scenario. We'll set it up the way we want it."

Norah couldn't keep silent. "He'll suspect."

Deland overrode her. "Of course he will, naturally. He'll suspect a trap, but we're going to make the intended victim so appealing, so much like Thelma Harrison, that he won't be able to resist." Deland removed the unlit cigar on which he'd been chewing relentlessly, regarded it with distaste, and set it aside in an ashtray, which already held three such mangled discards. "Personally, my opinion is that this last homicide at the Sixty-eighth Street station was a direct response to the trap we set at the other station." Deland paused.

His only response was silence.

"Gorin picked up our challenge and outwitted us. The contest has added an extra dimension to the high he gets when he kills."

"All the more reason to believe he'll respond to a well-chosen decoy," Aspen said.

Deland had indicated to Norah that she was no longer in charge, but quite obviously she was not off the case. She felt the first flush of excitement. "I'm a little taller than Thelma Harrison and she was a little plumper than me, but in flats and a loose coat that won't be noticeable. I could wear tinted contacts and our hair is the same shade. I'll have mine styled like hers. I could wear a nurse's uniform, or would that be too much?"

There was an awkward silence. She sensed it, of course; she could hardly miss it, but didn't understand what it meant. It was Jim Felix who explained.

"Thelma Harrison was twenty-two years old."

Still she didn't get it.

"The decoy should not only be about the same age, she

should appear . . . vulnerable," Deland added. "You're a very competent woman, Norah. It shows. There's an aura that I believe this perpetrator is not likely to miss. I doubt he'd attack you."

In trying to make it better, the chief had made it worse, Norah thought. She was too old, that was what he meant. That was the nub of it. Too old. Her cheeks grew hotter. She was blushing. She was mortified on both counts.

"Do you have someone in mind?" She shouldn't have asked, but she couldn't help herself, and surely her work on the case and having brought it this far gave her the right.

Felix replied, "As a matter of fact, we do. Officer Webber."

Norah caught her breath. Somehow, she'd known.

"She resembles Harrison, don't you think?"

Norah could have pointed out the dissimilarities, but it wouldn't have made any difference. She went to the core. "Webber hasn't been on the force six months."

"She participated in the canvass for Todd Millard and turned important information."

Her partner did that, Norah thought, but didn't say it.

"She also took part in the first subway stakeout and ac-quitted herself . . ." Felix searched for the right word. "Cred-itably. You were there; would you agree?"

"Yes. As part of the crowd. You're planning to make her the focus of all attention." Norah took a breath. "She's not ready," she stated flatly, determined to maintain a profes-sional attitude. After all, what she said was true.

"Under the circumstances, her lack of experience may be an advantage," Deland suggested. "She'll act more like a civilian." So they'd decided. Might as well get to the bottom line, Norah thought, getting to her feet. "Am I to participate at all?"

"Of course," Deland assured her. "You're on the case till it's cleared," he announced formally.

"Thank you." Norah looked toward the door but waited till the chief indicated she was excused. She went to the anteroom and waited for the meeting to break up. Then she approached Jim Felix.

"May I speak with you for a moment?"

He led the way down the corridor to his office. He opened the door for her and followed her in. Then he closed the door.

"What's bothering you, Norah?"

"This is a very dangerous assignment Kathryn is taking on."

"Granted, but it is part of the job."

"If anything goes wrong, how is Sally going to take it?"

"Sally knows it's part of the job."

Norah clenched her jaw. Then she made up her mind. "Was Kathryn selected or did she volunteer?"

"She volunteered." Felix paused. "She asked for the assignment," he went on. "She's ambitious, eager to get ahead. Think back to your own early days, Norah. You volunteered for everything whether you had the qualifications or not. You were very pushy."

"Was I?" Norah smiled ruefully. "I'd forgotten."

"It was what made you stand out."

"Now I feel as though I'm being left behind."

"We all go through that. The truth is the opposite; you're moving on to other things, more important things. Kathryn's future is ahead of her. And so is yours."

"Thanks, Jim." Norah held out her hand.

Felix took it. "About Kathryn; she is more of a schemer than you were and more ruthless, but she doesn't mean any harm. I'd appreciate it if you would help her. Give her a few tips. She admires you."

She wished he hadn't asked. It drove the knife deeper. But she couldn't say no, not to Jim Felix.

"You have a lot to give, Norah."

"I'll do what I can," she said. She couldn't wait to get out of there.

She might still be on the case of the subway killer as Louis Deland had firmly asserted largely, Norah suspected, to make a point with Chief Woitach, but she had not been given any new assignment; actually she had been told to keep hands off. That suited her fine, she thought, just fine. It was not her type of operation—big task force, massive search, intricate deployment of armed men. The numbers would reassure the public but might frighten the perpetrator. She was more comfortable working with a small team.

In those first days of December, the weather continued to be balmy. Accustomed to long, beneficent autumns, New Yorkers were beginning to complain at the unseasonal warmth; the flu was rampant. Norah, however, had no fault to find with the weather. Having left police headquarters, she bought a hot dog from a sidewalk vendor in Foley Square, found a bench, and sat down, stretching her legs out in front of her and letting the sun caress her face and warm her whole body as she munched.

She made no direct attempt to channel her thoughts, rather let her subconscious lead her, and thus she found herself dwelling again on the Danay case, particularly on the parents of the kidnapped child. It occurred to her that she knew very little about them. Respecting their sorrow and shock, she had not pressed them. Now that time had passed and the initial impact worn off, she should talk to them again, not for any particular reason but because the better the understanding she had of the various relationships, the more chance of interpreting what had happened. Adele Millard had shown no eagerness to talk to Norah. She had told her to call her secretary for an appointment, which meant she preferred to meet her in the formal atmosphere of the office. Norah decided not to read anything into that, yet. She hadn't got round to making the appointment. Now was a good time.

But she didn't move from the bench.

She had spent even less time with Todd's father. None with Professor Millard's second wife, Louise. How did Louise feel about all this? The renewal of bonds between her husband and his former wife and his son must distress her. Parental kidnapping had been suggested, Norah recalled, and she had dismissed it. Had she been too quick?

So now Norah got up, found a phone booth, and called the squad.

Ferdi answered. "Lieutenant, I've been trying to get you. Mrs. Millard called. She's very anxious to talk to you. She wants you to call her right away. At her office."

"Did she say what it's about?"

"Just that it's urgent."

"All right. What's the number? Oh, and better give me the address, too. I might go over."

"You want somebody to meet you there?"

Norah was as sensitive to Ferdi's hunches as he was to hers. Nor did she dismiss them lightly. So she waited a couple of seconds and considered. "No," she decided. "Not this time."

The offices of Hammer, Prescott, Millard were not particularly impressive, Norah thought as she entered the plain building lobby at street level. The edifice on Madison Avenue was traditionally tenanted by advertising firms whose prestige did not depend on glitzy decor but rather on a record of solid performance. Upstairs, the reception room of the firm was similarly low key. Hammer, Prescott, Millard was indeed secure in its reputation. Norah identified herself to the mature receptionist. Within moments, a slightly younger but still not by any means glamorous secretary appeared to escort Norah to Adele Millard's sanctum. Her name in small letters and without title was discreetly displayed on the door, suggesting those who sought her already knew her importance.

Adele Millard got up and stretched out a hand.

"You needn't have troubled to come over, Lieutenant."

She was very composed, Norah thought, very much "in charge," as though she'd occupied that office and sat in that big chair for a very long time.

"You did say it was urgent."

"Yes, it is." Waving Norah to the client's chair, Adele Millard sat down again. "I'm going on television tonight. CBS has a new show. It's a cross between 'Forty-eight Hours' and 'Unsolved Mysteries.' They're calling it 'Neighborhood Hot Line.' It will air once a month and is being introduced tonight. Tonight's segment deals with the disappearance of children. It reviews old cases, some of which have been solved and some of which remain a mystery. I'm being given the opportunity to appeal for information regarding Todd." Her dark eyes filled. Her face, though impassive, revealed the pain behind the mask.

"I want my son back. I'm offering twenty-five thousand dollars for information leading to his return. No questions asked."

"That's a lot of money," Norah said. "I don't mean to pry, but after paying the ransom . . ."

"You wonder where I'm getting it?"

"Yes."

"From the estate. Peter Bouchard feels he has the right to authorize whatever monies are necessary to get Todd back. The entire intent of my mother's will is to protect and nurture Todd."

"And your husband, your ex-husband," Norah corrected herself. "Will he appear on the show with you?"

"Of course."

* * *

The appearance of Adele and Richard Millard came at the very end of the program, which was an advantage to them since it left their appeal fresh in the viewer's mind. The two were presented sitting on a small settee side by side, their hands clasped. They looked directly into the camera, their strain and sorrow clearly evident. They were ill at ease and that added to the poignancy. Adele did most of the talking, saying the things she had said to Norah earlier in her office. She concluded, tears in her eyes, as the camera closed in:

"Please, if you know anything about my son, if you have any idea where he is, please call. I'll bless you every day for the rest of my life."

Her voice broke. She couldn't continue.

Millard took over. "Todd, if you can hear my voice—we love you. Your mother and I have never stopped loving you." He took the woman beside him into his arms to comfort her.

And how did the current Mrs. Millard, if she was watching and she must be, Norah thought, feel about that?

As the picture of the grieving couple started to fade, the face of the boy was superimposed. At the bottom of the screen, the legend in yellow letters:

HAVE YOU SEEN THIS CHILD?

In grave tones, the narrator gave a detailed discription of Todd and then advised the public what number to call if they had any information.

Norah turned off her set.

Chapter SIXTEEN

The switchboard at the local CBS station and the switchboards of the affiliates across the nation that had carried the show lit up before it went off the air. The calls offered sympathy and support for the Millards and commendation to the network for airing the story and the Millards' appeal. Information along with claims to the reward money swamped the lines. Children corresponding to Todd's description were reported spotted in states from New York to California. He was living with a family in the same building as the man who called from Brooklyn. He was attending school with the son of the caller in Stroudsburg, Pennsylvania. He was being held, chained in a chicken coop, on a farm in West Virginia; the caller, a rural mailman, had recognized him while on his rounds. No matter how unlikely, or even absurd, the operators took it down. Every account would be turned over to the police and the tedious job of checking would begin. Meanwhile, Norah pursued her own line of investigation.

Early the next morning, she drove to Stamford and the Millards' house. Driving against traffic, she made good time and was there shortly after nine. She parked in the driveway and walked up a curving path to ring the doorbell of the ranch-style house. She waited a considerable time, but she was certain someone was at home because there was a car in the garage. At last the door opened.

"Mrs. Millard?"

The woman had a pretty face, but it was puffy and there were dark discolorations under her pale blue eyes. She looked as though she were about to give birth right there at the door. No wonder it had taken her so long to answer.

"Are you all right?"

Louise Millard shrugged. "I'm uncomfortable, impatient, but in the sense you mean—sure, I'm okay." She held onto the door frame to maintain her balance.

Norah was not convinced. "I could take you to the hospital."

"Who are you?"

"Oh, I'm sorry. Lieutenant Mulcahaney, New York Police." She showed her open shield case. "I'm investigating Todd Millard's disappearance. We haven't met, but I've talked with your husband."

"Yes, he told me." Louise Millard swayed slightly.

Norah reached out a hand. "Let's go in and sit down."

"Thanks. Standing isn't the greatest."

Leaning on Norah's arm, Louise Millard waddled into the living room, which opened off a central hall to the right, and then crossed to the sofa, lowering herself into it with care and finally a sigh of accomplishment.

"I wish I could get this done and over with. I'm two weeks overdue."

"You'll forget all about the discomfort and the pain once the baby is here."

"That's what they tell me."

"I guess your husband feels the same way."

"Not exactly," Louise Millard muttered and then grinned. So did Norah. "Is he at home?"

The smile faded. The light blue eyes seemed to dim. "He's in New York. With her. He went up to be on that television show. He was supposed to come right back."

At a loss what to say, Norah remained silent.

"I don't know what's going on!" the mother-to-be burst out. "I don't. That woman has Richard on a string. First, she didn't want him. She didn't like being a professor's wife. It wasn't glamorous enough. She wanted a career like her mother had. So she got a divorce. *She* got it, right? Women all over the world get divorces. They don't want to be wives and mothers. It's not fulfilling. Fine. It's their decision, but leave those of us who pick up after them and who are satisfied with their discards, leave us alone.

"The trouble with Adele is she hasn't got the talent to make it on her own. She's no actress, but she has a flair for salesmanship; got it from her father. So, she set up her own shop with her mother paying for it. With her mother's money to back her and her mother's promise to come out of retirement and appear as narrator in a drama anthology series of television shows, Adele should have had it made. Right? Wrong. She started by wasting money on fancy offices and a big staff. The networks were interested; why wouldn't they be with the anticipation of the return of the legendary Wilma Danay? But they had reservations about the script. They wanted changes. Apparently, Adele was impatient. She wouldn't take the time to do what they wanted and instead went ahead and produced the pilot on her own. It flopped. Even with Wilma as part of the package, nobody wanted it and her money was gone."

"She bought into Hammer, Prescott."

"That's right, she did, again with her mother's money. Wilma gave her a second chance, but she made sure in the will there wouldn't be a third. She didn't want her money to be thrown away. So if she doesn't make a go of it this time,

Adele is finished. Yolanda can't help her, and she's not getting Richard back. I can promise you that."

"When you say Yolanda can't help her, what do you mean?"

"Just that. For almost all of Adele's life, Yolanda has given her the love, comfort, and nurturing Wilma was too busy to supply. The two of them, Adele and Yolanda, have supported each other, protected each other from Wilma's turbulence, from her outbursts. Yolanda was a true mother to Adele. She would do anything for her, give her anything, except money. Only because she doesn't have any."

A grimace of pain passed over Louise Millard's face.

"Are you all right?"

"I think so."

"I'm going to take you to the hospital."

"No. It's not time. Not yet." Louise Millard closed her eyes. After several moments, she opened them again. "But soon . . . maybe . . ."

"Do you want me to call your husband?"

"No!" The answer was immediate and positive. "I don't want him to be coerced or shamed into . . ." She gritted her teeth at the new wave of pain. "Yes, yes. Please. Call him. Tell him to come. Tell him I need him."

"Where is he staying?"

"At her place."

That number didn't answer. Next, Norah tried the Danay apartment and got Yolanda Yates.

"This is Lieutenant Mulcahaney. Is Professor Millard there?"

He answered promptly.

"I'm with your wife, Professor. She needs you. Right away."

"Oh? Oh, my God! Yes, I'm coming. Right now. Immediately." His response indicated relief. He sounded as though he welcomed the summons, as though he was glad to be forced to return.

Norah made arrangements with a neighbor to sit with Louise Millard and headed back to the city. She would talk with the professor later. Now her first priority was to get an order allowing her to examine the bank records pertaining to Wilma Danay's account. Probably Peter Bouchard would be able to give her the information she needed, but Norah didn't trust him and anyway, she was after more than mere recollection. She wanted facts and confirmation of the facts that she now perceived to be at the core of a shocking crime that had gone out of control. She wanted to make absolutely certain of what was and was not, and she was willing to take all the time needed. The case had started with a tremendous sense of urgency because of the imminent danger to the missing boy. That was past. Whatever had happened to Todd had happened; it couldn't be changed. Nevertheless, Norah was impatient and once she had the legal authorization, she wasted no time getting over to Wilma Danay's bank. She took Julius Ochs, an expert in such matters, along with her. She would be searching for something she didn't expect to find. Its absence would support the positive evidence.

Norah now believed she knew what had happened Sunday night after the bridge game. In the commission of one crime, another had been perpetrated, both as cruel and heartless as any she'd ever dealt with. It disgusted her that the instigator didn't have the guts to do his own bloody work. Norah had often wondered how a heretofore law-abiding citizen went about hiring a killer. He couldn't call an agency or put an ad in the paper. In this case, the prospective employer hadn't had to look for a hired hand. One known to the members of Wilma Danay's small, elite circle was available.

Once again Norah visualized the terrible struggle between the aged star and her assailant. She imagined the child cowering in his room, listening to his grandmother's cries for help and bravely calling 911, then watching as the door was kicked in. For a moment child and assailant faced each other frozen in uncertainty. Which one moved first? Todd? Looking across the hall into his grandmother's moonlit bedroom and seeing her motionless on the floor, Todd must have known instinctively that she was dead. At that moment he also knew he had to save himself.

Beating an old woman was bad enough, but how could anyone subject a child to such terror and confusion, especially someone who claimed to care for him? Norah thought again of Adele Millard's television appeal. It had been addressed to the public at large—apparently. Could it have been directed at a specific person? A terrible chill crept over Norah.

She requested another meeting with Adele, who though reluctant, couldn't refuse. It was to take place at the Danay apartment, and Norah asked Yolanda Yates to be present also. She wanted the occasion to be dignified; at least to start that way. Julius Ochs was therefore instructed regarding the image he should present. Instead of his usual jeans and sports jacket, Julie Ochs wore a three-piece suit and produced granny glasses when it came to the close work, though he didn't really need them. He also carried a briefcase with copies of the records he and Norah had spent the last three days studying. Norah wore a suit of soft Irish tweed with a skirt rather than pants and carried her good saddle leather shoulder-strap handbag—a new acquisition to accommodate her police special and her new reading glasses—which she did need, very much.

Admitting them, Yolanda Yates was subdued and ushered them to the salon where Adele Millard waited. She was seated at a wide window looking out toward the Queensboro

Bridge and well away from the dominating influence of her mother's portrait. It had been dark since five and the soft December night wrapped itself around the city, cradling it. Inside the salon, the lights were low to enhance the spots focused on the individual paintings. She hadn't realized there were so many, Norah thought. They were hung so close it was almost impossible to discern the pattern of the wallpaper underneath. And these were genuine!

Having introduced Detective Ochs, Norah settled herself opposite the two women, and Ochs pulled up a chair to the coffee table and began to lay out the documents.

"These are photocopies of the bank records pertaining to Miss Danay's account over the past five years. Additional copies will be made available to you, if you so desire."

"If either of you has any knowledge of any other bank with which Miss Danay might have done business, now would be a good time to tell us," Norah said and waited.

Both women shook their heads.

"All right, I will now ask each of you certain questions to which we already know the answers."

"Then why . . ." Adele Millard began.

Norah raised a hand. "Bear with me. Your mother, Wilma Danay, gave you a large sum of money approximately sixteen months ago. It was, in fact, your inheritance. She gave it to you in advance because you asked her to. You needed it to go into business. Is that right?"

"Yes."

"But the project didn't go well. In fact, you went bankrupt. Is that right?"

Millard nodded.

"The money was used up. You asked for more but your mother refused."

"What are you getting at?"

"Your mother refused, didn't she?"

Adele Millard's dark eyes narrowed. The taut skin of her face seemed about to crack. At that moment, she looked very much like Wilma Danay, Norah thought.

"You begged and pleaded, but your mother was adamant. You had a big opportunity to buy into a prestigious advertising firm, you told her. But it was no use. Your mother was intolerant of failure."

"I don't see that this has anything to do with the investigation, Lieutenant."

"It has everything to do with it. I wish it weren't so."

Adele Millard pursed her lips in annoyance. "Get to the point then, Lieutenant."

"All right. Where did you get the five hundred thousand to buy into Hammer, Prescott?"

"My mother gave it to me. First, she said no, then she changed her mind."

"Not according to the bank records. The statements show a withdrawal of the initial gift of one million on June thirtieth of last year. The canceled check shows your signature as endorsement. There is no record of any other large withdrawal and no other canceled check bearing your endorsement in any amount, large or small." Before Millard could speak, Norah added, "Do you now recall any other bank your mother might have used?"

"No."

"Then where did the half million for Hammer, Prescott come from?"

"I repeat, it's none of your business." Despite her words, there was little defiance left in Adele Millard.

"I didn't ask you *who* gave you the money. I asked you where it came from."

"And I told you." She managed to meet Norah's eyes.

"A woman who uses her own child, her flesh and blood, as an instrument for extortion deserves no pity."

"What are you talking about?"

"Everyone I've spoken with, everyone who was close to you and your mother tells me the same thing; the two of you did not get along. Your attitudes were opposed; your philosophies clashed. You fought about everything. Constantly, almost inevitably, you did what she didn't want you to do. You quit school when she wanted you to stay and graduate. You married one of your professors against your mother's wishes. By the time she adjusted and accepted the marriage, you decided to get a divorce. The only thing you achieved of which she approved was giving birth to Todd. Your son, Todd, was the joy of your mother's life. She doted on him. It was for his sake she opposed the divorce. When, despite her admonitions, you went ahead anyway, she would have taken Todd in to live with her, but she believed it would not have been in his best interests. He should be, if not with both, at least with one of his parents.

"Your mother had worked hard for her money," Norah went on. "She expected that outsiders, tradespeople, hustlers of all kinds, would try to take advantage of her. Even those closest to her wanted something. When a friend asked for help, Wilma Danay listened sympathetically and gave it— once. Once only—that was her rule and it applied to you too. And you knew it. She had given you your inheritance, and you knew there wasn't a chance in the world of getting any more. But the rule didn't apply to Todd. Todd wasn't likely to ask his Nana for a half a million dollars, but someone could do it on his behalf."

"No!"

"A fake kidnapping was set up. Naturally, someone was hired to make the snatch. To be sure you had a solid alibi you went to Chicago to meet with your new partners and waited to be notified. As soon as you were, you came running back, eager to pay the ransom."

"Of course I was eager to pay the ransom."

"You couldn't wait to pay it."

"I wanted my son."

"You didn't want any police presence when you turned the money over."

"That's right, I didn't. How many times has the presence of the police frightened the kidnapper or made him so angry that as a result the child was not recovered?" she demanded.

"It happened this time."

Norah was not impressed. She raised her strong, square chin. "You sit in a large, dignified office and your name is on the door, Hammer, Prescott, Millard. Therefore, I assume you paid your entry fee. What happened to Todd?"

"You aren't seriously suggesting . . .? You're wrong. I swear to God, you're wrong!"

"When he took the shopping bag from you in the street, I assume your hired hand kept what was in it as his share. So why wasn't the boy returned?"

"I don't know. I keep telling you I had nothing to do with it. Please. This is outrageous."

"As executor of your mother's will, Peter Bouchard authorized payment to you of the balance of the ransom, but that still left you short to fulfill your contract with Hammer, Prescott."

Putting her hands to her ears to shut out anything else Norah might say, Adele Millard got up and stalked to the far side of the room. "Go away. Leave me alone."

Yolanda Yates jumped up and followed. She put her arms around Adele Millard, patting, cooing, trying to comfort her. "Baby, baby, it's all right. It's all right."

"I had nothing to do with it. You tell her. Tell her."

The companion continued to hold her, stroking her dark hair gently. She looked over her head to Norah.

"I gave her the money."

It was the admission toward which Norah had been working, but she felt little satisfaction.

"Where did you get it?"

"I saved it over a period of years."

"That's a lot of money even for the magic of compounded interest," Norah remarked dryly.

"You didn't let me finish," Yates snapped. "I made some good investments. From time to time, Mr. Bouchard gave me tips. I gave him what money I had and he invested it for me through his broker."

"Peter Bouchard lost just about everything he had in the market."

"Actually, it was Wilma who gave me the tips."

"She pulled out of the market well before the crash of eighty-seven. She didn't even dabble after that."

"But she continued to follow the market and chart it," Yolanda insisted. "Wilma was fanatically interested. She told me what stocks she thought would go up and which ones were dangerous. She played the market on paper like some people play the horses, without ever placing a bet. And she was amazingly correct. She had no idea I was listening and playing for real."

"Somebody had to handle your transactions. Who's your broker?"

"I told you. I worked through Pete Bouchard."

Norah dropped it, temporarily. "How was the money turned over to you?" she asked Adele Millard. "By check? In cash? In a Bloomingdale's shopping bag?"

"No, Addie, no! I didn't do it. I'm not responsible." Yates was quick to defend herself. "You can't believe I would do such a thing. I couldn't have. Don't you remember? I was in Montreal with my sister. I got a call saying Isabel had been in an automobile accident. I told you that. Addie? Baby? You know I went up there. You know it, too, Lieutenant."

She was ever more desperate. "You talked to my sister on the phone. She verified I'd been there and was headed back. I have my ticket. I have my reserved seat ticket . . ."

"But your sister had not been in an accident," Norah pointed out. "The hospital had no record of having Isabel as a patient or of making a call to you. I remember that, too."

"It was a mixup. That happens."

"Or else there never was any such call. You made it up as an excuse to be away when the kidnapping took place."

"I say I got a call; you say I didn't. Neither one of us has any proof. In fact, it seems to me that your entire case is based on things that didn't happen or aren't there. Mrs. Millard and I have been patient and cooperative. She's lost a mother and a son. I've lost the friend of a lifetime and I loved Todd dearly. Enough is enough. I think you and your detective should leave."

"After you tell me where you got the money you claim you turned over to Mrs. Millard."

The companion's angular face was set grimly. "I did not get it by hiring someone to kidnap Todd." Her face softened with the tenderness reserved for Adele Millard only. "I had nothing to do with his kidnapping or with Wilma's death," she assured her. Then she turned back to Norah. "That's all I'm going to say."

Norah debated within herself; should she arrest Yolanda Yates right now? There was certainly probable cause. On the other hand, if she left her free . . .

"When's the last time you were in contact with Henry Lancelot?"

Chapter
SEVENTEEN

"I don't know if I did right to mention Lancelot," Norah wondered as she and Ochs walked along the austere, marbled lobby. A white-gloved doorman anticipating their pace opened the plate-glass door for them just as they reached it. The building with its cobblestoned courtyard and pebbled garden was set well back from the street and formed a small alcove of privilege within which the usual city noises were faint, if they could be heard at all. The dominant sound was the rhythmic rise and fall of the fountain in the center, a soothing pattern. Norah and Julius Ochs headed to the foot of the drive where Norah had parked her car.

"It was worth a try," Ochs responded.

In fact, Norah had planned the interrogation confidently, constructing it so that at the mention of Yolanda Yates's long-ago lover, one or the other of the women would break.

"Adele was a little girl, eight or nine years old, when Henry Lancelot came into Yolanda's life," Norah rationalized. "She probably knows the story, but not necessarily the name. As for Yates, Henry Lancelot was the love of her life. He mesmerized her to the point where she turned over Wilma Danay's jewels to him and replaced them with copies. He was the only man who ever showed a romantic interest in her. His hold was so strong that she betrayed a woman who was good to her and to whom she was devoted. She's been living in the shadow of that betrayal for years. The name should have evoked some kind of reaction, but she remained absolutely stolid."

"That's a reaction of a kind," Ochs pointed out.

"True."

Together they crossed the street and walked over to the car in which Arenas and Neel were waiting.

Norah shook her head. "Neither one of them took the bait. So the next step is to get hold of Bouchard's broker. Tomorrow. No, tomorrow's Sunday. Make it Monday." She would not be taking Sunday off, but the broker would. And the next subway stakeout was scheduled for Monday, but that would be late afternoon and neither of the men here would be involved. She, herself, wouldn't have much to do.

"So, on Monday, Julie, you get over to Bouchard's broker and sort out the transactions since eighty-seven: trades, profits, losses, withdrawals. See if you can separate Bouchard's from Yates's. That shouldn't be too hard."

"Right."

"Any word from Simon?" Wyler was covering Henry Lancelot.

Ferdi Arenas replied, "Lancelot left for work at five-thirty. We haven't heard since."

She frowned. Tracing the actor had been routine. The obvious first step had been to look him up in the telephone directories of the five boroughs. Next they checked the unlisted numbers. After that, Ferdi had gone through the records of Con Ed; nobody could exist without electricity. There was the possibility that he was using another name or living in a sublet or a hotel. He could have left the city, of course, but that was the worst scenario. Why assume the worst? In fact, their optimism was rewarded: they located him through Social Security. Henry Lancelot was currently employed as a waiter in a restaurant in the Village, The Gazebo.

"All right," Norah said. "Let's do it this way. Julie, you and Danny take his car and stay here to cover the two women upstairs." She indicated the lighted windows of the Danay apartment. "Ferdi and I will see if we can't catch up with Mr. Lancelot."

Ferdi made the call to the restaurant from a booth on Third Avenue while Norah stood beside him at the open door.

"Yes? Hello . . .? Is this The Gazebo? . . . I was wondering how late you serve dinner? . . . Till eleven. Good. Very good. We can certainly make that without any trouble. One more thing, you have a Henry Lancelot there? . . . Ah, Mr. Lance . . . Yes, he'd be the one. He served us very well the other night and we'd like to sit at one of his tables . . . Oh, I see. Well, that's too bad . . . Yes, we'll be coming anyway. Certainly . . . See you soon. Thank you." He hung up.

"Mr. Lance took sick suddenly and went home." Ferdi told Norah.

Her eyebrows rose. "Suddenly, after receiving a phone call, no doubt."

"He didn't say."

Norah took a deep breath and expelled it in an audible grunt like an athlete striving for maximum effort. "We can only hope," she said, and they went back to the car.

Henry Lancelot lived conveniently near his place of work on a tree-lined street of brownstones that had the quiet aura of the past, when on a soft night like this people strolled outdoors and ate ice cream and looked up to the stars. It was still early on a Saturday night, but no one was out.

She parked at the end of the block and then along with Ferdi walked back to where Simon Wyler had taken a position at a bus shelter.

"He's up there." Wyler indicated a pair of lighted windows on the top floor of a brownstone across the street. They were curtained, but the light showed through. "Apartment 5A."

"What about the back?"

"There's a service door at basement level. The super opens it once at five A.M. for the trash collection. He keeps it locked and bolted for the rest of the time and he has the only key."

Norah felt the blood course faster, a tingling sensation. A break was imminent. Arenas and Wyler sensed it, too.

"Wait for us," she told Wyler.

She hadn't really expected to apprehend Yolanda Yates's lover. He should have skipped long since. He should have taken the money and run as he had taken the jewels and run all those long years ago. But criminals were not known for rationality. So, it appeared luck was with them again, Norah thought, and she intended to take full advantage. Instead of pushing the bell for 5A, she rang the one marked *Super*. After a short wait, a tubby, balding man of about sixty in clean chinos and well-worn cardigan, appeared at the other side of the glass see-through panel to look them over.

"Can't be too careful who you let in these days, Officers," he apologized, having closely scrutinized both their IDs.

"Absolutely, Mr . . .?"

"Hazen. Duane Hazen."

"I wish there were more like you, Mr. Hazen," Norah commended. "We're here to talk to one of your tenants, Henry Lancelot. Has he lived in the building a long time?"

"Ever since I can remember and I've been here . . . thirty years."

"He's lived here all that time without interruption?"

"What do you mean—without interruption?"

"I mean, has he been away for any length of time? Does he travel?"

"Oh sure, yes. He travels a lot. Sometimes he's away for extended periods, even months. Once he was away for over a year. He's an actor, you know."

"Is that so?"

"Yes. If he gets a job in a movie or television, he has to go wherever they're shooting. He's been all over the world."

"And he continues to maintain the apartment."

"Sure. It's rent-controlled."

"Ah. Still, he must make a lot of money."

"Actors don't make as much as people think. You'd be surprised. Also, they don't work steady. Show business is tough; it's feast or famine. Like now, things aren't so good for Lance. He's working as a waiter in a restaurant around the corner."

Assuming that her reconstruction of the crime was correct and that they had the right man and it was Henry Lancelot who had snatched the boy and then picked up the ransom from Adele Millard, by staying on and maintaining his regular life-style, he was showing a lot of discipline. Or foolhardiness, Norah thought.

"When was the last time Mr. Lancelot was away for an extended period?"

Hazen thought about it. "He was away early this year from, say late March to the end of June. He's not in any trouble, is he? I can't believe he can be in any trouble. Everybody likes Lance." Hazen smiled indulgently. "Particularly the ladies. He goes out of his way to be nice and to do them favors: Run down to the store, mail a letter, like that. Best of all, he flatters them, makes them feel like girls again."

"How do their husbands like that?"

"Most of them are widows or spinsters. But he gets along with the men, too. We have a weekly poker game, and if he's around and not working either at the restaurant or shooting a picture, he plays with us. He's pretty good."

"Bluffs a lot?"

"Now that I think of it, yeah." Hazen beamed. "He's an actor, after all."

The elevator was out of order. By the time they climbed to the fifth floor, Norah was out of breath, lungs burning. Her legs ached. Ferdi, however, showed no sign of discomfort. She was ten years older and it was beginning to tell. She took a position to one side of the door and Ferdi the other. With a nod she indicated he should ring the bell.

"Yes? Who is it?" The voice from behind the door was deep, pleasantly modulated but wary.

"Police officers, Mr. Lancelot," Ferdi Arenas replied easily. "Like to talk to you for a few minutes."

"What about?"

"Your friend Yolanda Yates," Norah said.

There was a short pause, then the rattle of the chain and the snap of the bolt. The door opened partway.

He was not at all what Norah had expected. She had envisioned a Quentin Noble, slim, aesthetic, with a sharp-edged profile. Or perhaps a Peter Bouchard, before he'd put on the weight, eyes hooded and full, sensuous lips. Sleek and slick. A Rudolf Valentino or John Gilbert, dark and exotic. Those were the stars of Wilma Danay's time. Lancelot was big, almost hefty; six feet and close to two hundred pounds. He lacked polish, yet there was a sultry, sexy quality about him.

She took a quick look around the small, high-ceilinged room. There was a convertible couch—open, the bed clothes in a pile at the foot. It faced a wall of bookcases and storage cabinets. The plaster on the flanking walls was badly water-damaged, probably the result of leaks from the roof. A few minor repairs and a good paint job and it could be a pleasant place, Norah thought, her eyes resting on a pair of suitcases near the kitchen door.

"Going somewhere, Mr. Lancelot?"

"A short trip, yes."

"Unexpected?"

"Yes, that's right. I got a call tonight just a short while ago about a job. Up at Lake George. There's that big new hotel, uh . . . the Sagamore. Actually, it's an old hotel done over. They're going to run one of those mystery weekends. You've heard about them?"

"I have."

"I'll play one of the characters in the story. It's mostly improvisation. They don't pay much, but it's fun. You get away for a couple of days, live elegantly, eat well, are treated with respect. Forget your troubles."

"That's what the call you got at the restaurant tonight was about?"

Lancelot looked hard at Norah, then at Arenas. He didn't ask how they knew where he worked or that he had received a phone call. He merely nodded.

Smart enough not to volunteer anything, Norah thought. "The call wasn't from your old friend Yolanda Yates, warning you to get out of town?"

"What?"

"I hope you're not going to waste our time and yours by pretending you don't know Yolanda Yates."

He frowned. "I know Yolanda."

"And you know why we're here."

"No, I don't. Honestly."

"Where were you the night of November eleventh at approximately ten-thirty P.M.?"

"I don't know. Working at the restaurant, I suppose."

"It was a Sunday. The restaurant isn't open on Sunday."

He shrugged. "You can't pull a date out of the air and expect me to remember where I was and what I was doing."

"Monday was Veterans Day. Does that help?"

"It doesn't mean a damn thing."

Norah sighed. "You should have prepared an alibi, Mr. Lancelot. Yolanda did. Of course, you didn't expect to come under suspicion, did you?"

"I don't know what you're talking about. I'll say this, whatever Yolanda did or didn't do is no business of mine. I haven't seen her in over twenty years."

"And you didn't part on good terms, did you?"

He didn't answer.

"Come on, Mr. Lancelot. Yolanda's told me the whole story."

"Then you don't need to hear it from me."

Suddenly, it struck Norah: had Yolanda told it all? Or had she kept a part of it back, or maybe presented it in a light that was favorable to herself?"

"Why don't you give me your version?"

"It's over and done with."

"All right then, let me tell you." Norah paused, arranging her thoughts, feeling her way. "Twenty years ago Wilma Danay proclaimed her retirement from pictures and moved from Hollywood to New York. Here she began to construct the legend of mystery on which some people contend her fame rests. It was her greatest role, beyond any of the parts she played on the screen."

"You've got that right."

The bitterness came from too deep down not to be personal, Norah thought.

"She bought the apartment on Sixty-fourth and took Yolanda Yates in to live with her."

No comment this time.

"By the way, how did you happen to meet Yolanda?" Norah was casual.

"In the supermarket. She asked me to reach up for a box of cat food from a high shelf. I obliged."

"And one word led to another?"

"We both had cats." His smile was almost disarming. It made him look younger anyway and gave credence to his reputation among the local ladies.

"Yolanda Yates was in her forties, not particularly attractive and far from rich. She could have had a dozen cats and you would have passed on. But then she happened to mention that she worked for Wilma Danay, actually lived with her. That interested you. You decided to cultivate Yolanda Yates so that through her you could get to Danay.

"Yolanda fell for you, hard," Norah continued. "She was completely under your spell. Nevertheless, when you first presented your scheme, she recoiled from it, but you had made her so sexually dependent that she couldn't risk losing you. So she agreed to pass you her employer's jewels, one or two pieces at a time. You could have copies made to replace the authentic pieces. When you had enough of the real jewelry, the two of you would go away together, you told Yolanda. You promised. And she believed you. It worked perfectly. Wilma didn't notice the switch at first. Before she did you were gone, but without Yolanda."

"That's ancient history, for God's sake! Who cares what happened way back then?"

"We do," Norah said.

The actor was stunned. He looked from one to the other, from Norah to Ferdi and back. Finally he laughed, albeit a little uncertainly. "You can't get me on something that happened twenty years ago. That's ridiculous."

"Not if we link it to a homicide and kidnapping that happened less than a month ago on a night Yolanda Yates has an alibi and you don't."

He stopped laughing. "I want a lawyer. I'm not saying another word till I see a lawyer. I know my rights."

"We'll get you one. You can speak to him at the precinct."

"I want him now. Here."

"Sorry, it doesn't work like that. This is not one of your mystery weekends, Mr. Lancelot. Read him his rights, Sergeant."

"Wait. Hold it. Suppose I tell you the whole story? What will you do for me?"

"I don't make deals, Mr. Lancelot. And I doubt there's anything you can tell me I don't already know. Stealing those jewels from Wilma Danay was probably the biggest mistake of your life, of both your and Yolanda's lives. Didn't you ever wonder why Wilma Danay let you get away with it?"

"She was embarrassed. She didn't want to appear in court."

"How about the insurance company?" Norah pressed. "They strongly suspected it was an inside job, but Wilma Danay went to Yolanda's defense. She protected her and in doing so, spared you. The insurance company paid and ostensibly that was the end of the matter."

"Right."

"But did you never wonder why you had such bad luck in your career? Why you never landed the big parts, the parts that could have boosted you to stardom? Or why, when you did get a strong role you were fired in rehearsal? Usually without explanation?" Norah pressed. "Didn't it occur to you that Wilma Danay was pulling the strings? I think it did. I think as the years passed and with them your chances of success, you recognized Wilma's vengeance was dogging you. You brooded on how to pay her back.

"Of course, you weren't fool enough to try to repeat what you had done. You found another way, but, as before, you needed help from the inside and you turned to Yolanda. Though Yolanda had remained with the star all those years, you guessed that Danay was as relentless in reminding her of what she owed as she had been in persecuting you. You figured Yolanda had been eating humble pie for twenty years and you would be offering her a chance to get out from under."

Norah paused.

"As it happened, Yolanda was looking for a way to get her hands on some money, so she was receptive to the kidnapping scheme. You didn't think you needed an alibi, but Yates, remembering how suspicion for the substitution of the jewels had fallen on her, made sure she set one up for herself. Frankly, after what you did to her the last time, I'm surprised she trusted you."

Norah paused. That had bothered her ever since she first began to suspect Yates was involved. But now, all at once, it was clear—why Lancelot hadn't brought his accomplice with him on the Sunday night: Yolanda was the accomplice and not only would she have been instantly recognized by both Danay and the boy, but she wasn't available Sunday night. Sunday night she was traveling down from Montreal. By Monday morning, alibi established, she was back and ready to play her part.

Norah's eyes remained fixed on Lancelot. "The fact is, she *didn't* trust you, so she made sure to be around when you picked up the ransom. She was the one driving the white compact you jumped into on Ninety-sixth Street, wasn't she?"

He didn't answer. Not a nerve in his face twitched. He was an actor like the rest of them, she thought, and so was Yolanda.

Yolanda, Norah realized, had deliberately picked a fight with Richard Millard so that she'd have an excuse to walk out and join Lancelot. By stepping in to smooth matters and suggesting she go to her room, Norah had played into her hands.

"On Sunday, November eleventh, you waited across the

street from Wilma Danay's building for the regular weekly bridge game to break up. You saw the Bouchards drive out of the basement garage and you waited for Nick Kouriades to leave. You began to worry that somehow you'd missed him. While you were wondering whether you should go ahead, you spotted him on the street. He hailed a cab, got in, and was gone. Feeling easier, even confident, you set about implementing your plan. First, you went around the corner and bought a pizza that you took with you to the service entrance. It was locked, of course, but you had a key provided by Yolanda. The pizza was just in case anybody should wonder what you were doing in the back halls or why you were using the service elevator. Yolanda also provided a key to the apartment in case Miss Danay didn't open the door to you. By the way, did she? Did she let you in?"

He didn't answer.

"I don't suppose it matters." Norah shrugged. "Did she recognize you?"

He didn't answer.

"That's a stupid question, isn't it?" Norah was self-deprecating. "You couldn't afford to have her recognize you. So you disguised yourself—put on a mask maybe at the last minute while you were waiting at her door. Sure, that makes sense.

"You didn't want trouble. All you wanted was to get in, grab the boy and get out again, no confrontation physical or otherwise. That way she wouldn't know with whom she was dealing. You could make the ransom demand and when the money was handed over you'd return the boy. Fast and clean. Am I right?"

He didn't take that bait, either.

Norah went on. "Unfortunately, Wilma Danay hadn't read your scenario; she didn't play her part. She resisted. She fought you. She kicked and scratched and screamed.

She defended herself and the grandson she loved with fury and desperation. She got hold of a kitchen knife and stabbed you. Where? Where did she cut you?"

Lancelot winced but gave no indication where he might have been wounded. Later, if he agreed to an examination, the scar would be one more link in the chain of evidence. If he didn't, the refusal would weigh against him.

"She was a frail, eighty-four-year-old woman. You're a big, hulking man half her age. You could have put a gag in her mouth and tied her up. You didn't have to throw her around like a bag of old bones. You didn't have to shatter her jaw."

Still no reaction.

"You didn't have to kill her."

He took a deep breath. "She had a heart attack. The papers said so."

"A heart attack for which you were directly responsible."

"I didn't have anything to do with it. I don't know what you're talking about."

Nevertheless, Norah's heart started to pound. Here it comes, she thought. She sensed that Lancelot was at the breaking point. She kept very still, not even daring to look in Ferdi's direction. But Lancelot said no more.

"Actually, her death was bad luck for you." Once again Norah noted a quickening in him, a nervous alertness and uncertainty. "For one thing, the ransom demand was to have been made on Miss Danay. She was the one with the money. With her gone, the money would not be readily available. Your demand had to be modified. You and your associate had to settle for a lot less than originally intended.

"But that's not the worst of it. In the struggle, she scratched you, Mr. Lancelot, and the scrapings of your skin were under her nails. She pulled your hair and strands of it were clutched in her fists. She stabbed you and your blood was on the knife and on the floor and on her clothes. Your blood, Mr. Lancelot, yours and nobody else's.''

Now, Norah thought. There was nothing more to add.

"It was an accident," Henry Lancelot mumbled. "I didn't mean to kill her." His voice rose. "She brought it on herself right from the beginning, way back. It was all her fault."

Norah let her breath escape softly. Up to that moment she hadn't even known she was holding it.

"I was in Hollywood working as a chauffeur for Paramount," he went on, justifying himself. "The big shots had their own cars and drivers, naturally; I drove for the visiting celebrities. I would go and pick them up at the airport and be at their disposal while they were in town, or fill in if any of the regulars got sick. That's how I met Wilma, not through Yolanda at the supermarket or anywhere else. At that point, Wilma had already been retired several years and was thinking of making a comeback. She was in Hollywood for a test, a wardrobe test they called it; actually, it was to see how she would photograph after all that time; she was no spring chicken even back then. Anyway, we took to each other right away and so we got together. All I wanted from her was a small part in the picture. One word from her would have done it. One little word, but she wouldn't say it. She refused. She said I wasn't good enough. I lacked talent. Hell, she'd been enjoying my talent for weeks! She said I couldn't excite an audience and I was beginning to bore her. So I walked out."

"*You* walked out?"

"That's right—me. From her bed into Yolanda's, and that's what she never forgave me."

Norah shook her head and Ferdi sighed. Lancelot remained wrapped up in his memories.

"So that night, Sunday night, when she started kicking and scratching, all of that and all the frustration, the years of failure, the bit parts in second-rate touring companies, industrial shows, off-off-off Broadway, exploded in my head. I retaliated. I hit her back as hard as I could. I didn't know she had a weak heart."

Norah waited, but it was evident he needed to be prompted. "What happened to the boy?"

For a moment it appeared Lancelot didn't know what Norah was talking about. "Oh, he locked himself in his room and wouldn't come out. I talked to him through the door. I told him his dad was waiting for him."

"You let him think his father had sent you?"

"He didn't buy it. I had to force the door."

"And then?"

"Then he ran. He was fast. He dodged around me and out to the backstairs. By the time we reached bottom, my head was spinning and my heart was racing. It's a wonder *I* didn't have a heart attack. I had to stop to catch my breath. By then, he was out on the street and turning the corner at Third. When I got to Third he was two blocks ahead at the subway entrance and disappearing down the stairs."

Norah and Ferdi looked at each other. They'd canvassed every store, restaurant, movie theater and building. Norah searched the shelters, the streets, and nobody had thought of the subway. Yet the subway was on everybody's mind and not only because of the recent killings. Seven hundred and twenty-two miles of track constituted a city below a city. People were carrying on an existence in those tunnels. They were a place of refuge; they were a network of danger.

"Did you go down after him?" Norah asked.

"Sure, but he was nowhere around. The platform was empty. He must have got on a train."

And God only knows where he went! Norah thought. "Did you ask the token clerk?"

"What would have been the use? He was gone."

"So when you demanded the ransom, you didn't have the boy?"

"No. I never had him."

Norah took a deep breath. "Read him his rights."

"Don't you understand?" Lancelot pleaded. "I never had him. I never laid a hand on him."

"Go on," she said to Ferdi.

"Wait a minute! Wait! The kidnapping wasn't even my idea. It was Yolanda's. From beginning to end, it was her idea. I didn't go looking for her. She came to me."

While Ferdi Arenas booked Henry Lancelot and accompanied him through the long, tedious process of arraignment, Norah contacted Neel and Ochs still outside the Danay apartment and told them to bring Yolanda Yates in. Under pressure, Yates and Lancelot would each damn the other, she thought. It was what they deserved. But the case wasn't cleared. It wouldn't be till they found Todd.

Where was he? What had happened to him?

Chapter
EIGHTEEN

As far as Norah knew, there had never before been a dress rehearsal for such an operation. SWAT teams, of course, held training exercises, and it was the SWAT commander, Lieutenant Brian Cashman, who had called for this drill.

A recently completed station of the Queens line was chosen as the practice site. Being at the end of the line, its closing would not greatly inconvenience the riding public and would require no advance announcement. According to Lieutenant Cashman, a couple of quick run-throughs would suffice. The station would be returned to service almost before anyone was aware that it had been closed.

The men and women of the NYPD and the Transit Police, all in plainclothes, crowded the platform. Some were assigned to keep an eye on the public who would be legitimately using the actual station and to make sure no one got in the way. Also, they were to be ready to step in if the suspect showed any intention to assault anyone other than the decoy. The core of the force was positioned within reach of the decoy.

Kathryn Webber sat on a bench, shoulders hunched forward. Every now and then a shiver passed through her. She was wearing a loose navy wool coat. Her shoes were white oxfords and her stockings were white. The hem of her white starched uniform showed below the coat. Obviously, she was a nurse. Her narrow face was paler than usual; her lips licked clean of lipstick. Dark shadows under her eyes indicated she hadn't been sleeping well. She looked young, vulnerable, and scared. A most likely victim, Norah was bound to admit, and though she still had doubts about the rookie's ability to handle the assignment, her heart went out to the young woman. Maybe there were others who had doubts about Kathryn's competence, Norah thought. Maybe that was why the rehearsal had been called.

Though it was the sound they'd all been waiting for, the roar galvanized everyone. It was followed by a rush of hot air and the headlights, which at first were mere pinpricks in the black tunnel, became in seconds blinding.

Kathryn Webber got up, walked over to the edge of the platform, and craned over it.

The designated perpetrator took three quick steps and, hands thrust out in front, pushed.

She might have screamed, but nobody heard her. In seconds, Kathryn Webber was down on the tracks. The perpetrator plunged into the crowd. The train screeched to a halt just short of the station.

Norah knew that the power had instantly been turned off so that there was no danger from the third rail. Just the same, she was shaking. So was everybody else.

A ladder was lowered and Officer Webber helped back up.

SWAT Commander Cashman came over. He was sweating.

"You were too near the edge," he chastised. "I don't want him to be able to push you over, just to try. Also, you didn't step forward soon enough."

"I stepped forward as soon as I heard the train," Webber argued, but her voice quavered.

"Listen harder. Be more alert." Cashman scowled. "And

stay at the far end of the platform. Let me explain once more. For the duration of the operation, all trains passing through the lower level of the station in question will respond to manually operated signals. Each will stop outside the station and wait for clearance. I will transmit the appropriate signal to the engineer who will transmit to the motorman: *caution,* meaning the suspect has been spotted and the train should not come more than a quarter of the way in; *normal,* the train should enter the station all the way but at half speed. All motormen are to be prepared to stop at a second's notice."

Webber was white. Norah wasn't sure if it was because of the chewing out—Cashman was venting some of his own anxiety—or because the full realization of her own danger had finally struck home.

Cashman raised the bull horn. "Okay, people. We'll try it again."

He wasn't much more pleased by the second attempt than he had been by the first.

"You're looking around," he criticized. "You're anticipating. You're giving it away."

"I'm trying not to," Webber flared.

"Nothing is going to happen to you. Believe me. But if you want to back out . . ."

"No. I can do it."

"It's up to you."

Kathryn Webber hesitated. For a moment it looked as though she might change her mind. Then she caught sight of Norah Mulcahaney in a group just behind Cashman. "I can do it."

Cashman was better pleased the next time and called off the exercise. The various teams dispersed and headed downtown for the real thing.

Except for Kathryn Webber. She was to be taken to New

York Hospital in time to mix with the staff leaving at the end of the day shift. A large number of nurses, attendants, and technicians would be taking buses on York Avenue heading east to transfer to various subways. Many got off at Third and walked down to the Sixtieth Street entrance of the N and R lines. Today, Officer Webber in her nurse's outfit would be among them. It was not known whether the suspect, Nathaniel Gorin, selected his victim at the last moment from among the crowd on the platform or whether he had been observing her for any time in advance. The first two victims had been regular passengers using that particular station. Helen Wyatt had been a visitor to the city. The last, Sarah Brownwell, was an occasional rider and, anyway, she had been attacked at the Sixty-eighth Street station. However, just on the chance that he might be watching, it was decided that having Webber arrive with a group of authentic hospital workers would add to her credibility.

Nathaniel Gorin had disappeared. A watch was being kept at his apartment, but he didn't return there. He didn't show up at his job, either. It was the purpose of the exercise to lure him into revealing himself. In the fourth killing, he had been forced out of his pattern, and so the tension within him had not been totally released. On this Monday, the fifth victim must be so right, so suited to his need, that he wouldn't be able to resist.

Brian Cashman came up to Norah and stood beside her while the various cars loaded and pulled out. He was big and beefy, red-faced and sandy-haired. A tough disciplinarian, he was careful not to demand more than it was within an officer's ability to give. He was openly worried.

"We're putting a lot of responsibility on that girl," he said, nodding in the direction of Kathryn Webber as she stood all alone on the corner waiting for her transportation. "Think she can do it?"

"First-night nerves, that's all. She'll be okay," Norah said. "Mind if I talk to her?"

"I wish you would."

Norah left him and walked over. "Hi."

"Hello, Lieutenant." Kathryn Webber managed a wan smile. She was very different from the girl at the graduation party; nothing like the rookie who had barged into the Danay apartment.

"Scared?" Norah asked. When she didn't answer, Norah went on, "You'll be well protected. Nothing's going to happen to you. They'll blow your cover rather than let you get hurt."

In fact, as Norah well knew, it was impossible to prepare for every eventuality. She thought of her own first assignment to decoy duty. She'd had a rendezvous with a suspected killer late at night at Riverside Park. There was no moon, the fog lay thick, and somehow she'd gotten separated from her backup. The suspect jumped her and dragged her to the river's edge and into the water. He held her under. In the heart of the city of concrete and steel, she had nearly been drowned.

"That doesn't mean you should be passive," Norah warned. "Try to relax. Let it happen, but be on guard. Remember, it's natural to be scared. The perp' expects you to be scared. He expects you to struggle, to resist. Go for his hair; pull it out by the roots, right out of his scalp. Kick him. Aim for the groin if you can. Hurt him. Really hurt him. The longer you struggle, the more time we have to grab him."

"Yes, ma'am."

"If you feel yourself going over, hang on to him, take him with you."

"Thank you, Lieutenant."

"I wish you'd call me Norah."

"When you did decoy work, Norah, were you scared?"

"You'd better believe it."

"Are you coming with us?"

She hadn't planned to. She had no specific part to play and it had seemed futile, a waste of time. For no reason she could pinpoint, she changed her mind.

"No, but I'll be there. Count on me."

The scene shifted to the lower level between Fifty-ninth and Sixtieth. By four P.M., everyone was in place.

Detectives, some a part of Juvelis's Transit team and some from Norah's Fourth Division Homicide squad who had interrogated Gorin before he was a suspect and therefore would be likely to recognize him, were stationed on the street at the subway entrances. Their job was to notify command below the instant he was spotted.

All but one staircase and one escalator had been closed off ostensibly for repairs. Once they made the suspect, they didn't want to lose him in the crowd of legitimate passengers using the station. As time passed and the peak of the rush hour loomed, the platform was jammed so that the decoy was almost lost. She stood near a pillar on the uptown side and well past the center. Each time at the sound of an approaching train she took a couple of steps toward the edge and peered out, then came back as though it was not the train she wanted. The police, men and women, around her were constantly shifting positions so that it seemed they were coming and going whereas in fact they were always close to her, close enough to grab any assailant.

Norah was farther back; call it an observer's post. She wasn't watching the decoy or her immediate backup. Norah's back was to Webber. She was sweeping the crowd in the same way the secret service did when protecting a dignitary.

She picked him out as he was riding down on the escalator—a homeless man in rags, face caked with dirt, hair covered by a dark wool cap. It was the way he scanned the crowd with pale blue eyes that had caught Norah's attention, as though he were searching; mostly the homeless kept their eyes down. Was this, could this be Gorin?

She watched him get off the escalator and lost him for a while. When she picked him up again he was five or six feet away from Kathryn Webber, separated from her by at least four civilians and two undercover cops. At the sound of another train approaching, Kathryn went through her drill; stepped forward to the edge and peered into the black hole. They had choreographed her movements and those of the police, but they had not been able to anticipate what the civilians around her would do. As Kathryn stepped forward, they moved to the sides around her to get a look, too, and as they separated they left an open space between Kathryn and the man in rags.

Norah stared in dismay. It was only for a moment, but it would be enough. She wanted to yell and warn the girl. She couldn't. It would spoil the elaborate sting. Anyway, Kathryn wouldn't hear her in the noise and confusion. *Kathryn! Watch out! He's right behind you. Watch out!* The words were in her head; the scream was silent, nevertheless, Kathryn Webber did turn. Out of instinct, perhaps. She turned and saw the tattered man, the rage in his eyes, hands outstretched as he pushed off on his right foot and hurled himself bodily at her.

She reacted naturally. Instinct had warned her and she reacted instinctively. She executed the one maneuver that could save her and her timing was perfect. As the suspect lunged, she stepped to one side. Propelled by his own momentum, the man went hurtling past her down to the tracks.

She'd lost her nerve.

Norah groaned. It was the one thing she should not have

done. Because of it they'd failed. All the elaborate precautions—gone for nothing. There had been no contact between the suspect and Webber. He hadn't touched her or spoken to her. They would not be able to prove intent. He could even argue that somebody had pushed *him*. Or he could claim that he had jumped in a suicide attempt.

Meantime, the programmed responses had been activated.

The train stopped short of the platform.

The power was shut off.

Four SWAT officers jumped down to the tracks.

There was nowhere for the suspect to run; the train blocked one end of the tunnel and the police the other. He let them seize him, cuff him, push and pull him up the ladder and back onto the platform. He had his rights read to him.

A futile formality and Kathryn Webber knew it, Norah thought, watching her. The arrest wouldn't stand. She'd blown it.

As the detectives hustled the suspect through the crowd, they passed Webber in her nurse's outfit. For the first time he resisted, dragging his feet and forcing them to stop so that he was face to face with her. His eyes glittered wildly out of his mud-covered face. Nathaniel Gorin straightened up to his full six feet, reared back, and spat.

Kathryn stood frozen. She didn't raise a hand to clean herself.

"I'll get you," he snarled. "You killed my mother. I'll get you the next time."

Relief swept over Norah. They had a case, after all.

Chapter
NINETEEN

The police moved out; power was restored; the trains resumed normal operation. The rush hour was long since over. Norah waited till the backup of passengers was cleared and only a handful waited on the platform.

This is what it must have been like on the Sunday Todd Millard, running for his life, came down here. Someone should have taken notice of him. Certainly the token clerk should have since the boy had no money and would have had to duck under the turnstyle. She sighed. The fact that no one had come forward to report the solitary child didn't mean he hadn't been there. It was possible, naturally, that Lancelot was lying, but Norah believed him. The story felt right.

Todd was smart and he had spunk. Hearing the sounds of violence and his grandmother's screams, he'd had the presence of mind and the initiative to call 911. Not bad for a ten-year-old. He'd locked his door and cringed behind it, waiting for help to arrive. After a while, the sound of the struggle stopped. His grandmother stopped screaming. In that ominous silence, the intruder spoke to the child, cajoled, tried to lure him out. It didn't work. Finally, the intruder forced the door.

Todd, looking across the hall into his grandmother's bedroom, saw her lying on the floor battered and bloodied and . . . still. In that instant he knew he had to save himself. He ran.

He was young and driven by terror. But Lancelot was desperate, too. He followed the boy down the backstairs of the building and into the street. Todd was well ahead of him. He yelled that the boy had stolen his wallet; maybe somebody would believe it and grab Todd. But Todd didn't give anybody a chance. He saw the subway entrance and saw the chance to make good his escape. By the time Lancelot got down to the platform, Todd was gone. He might have been hiding in the lavatory, or even on the ledge just beyond the platform, but the simple and logical answer was that he got on a train. After that, the possibilities were limitless.

This wasn't the first time Norah had tried to see things from Todd's point of view, but she did know a little more about him now, about his character and his situation. To whom could he turn? His mother was out of town and he didn't know how to reach her. Yolanda Yates, his grandma's companion, was also away. Obviously he didn't believe it when Lancelot told him his father, Richard Millard, was waiting for him. Nevertheless, a doubt had been planted so that later when he could get to a phone, he didn't try to contact his father. Nor did he call 911 a second time. That had bothered Norah from the start and still did.

She walked home slowly, thoughtfully. By the time she got there, Norah had a plan. There was a reporter for the *Post*, a man who had covered several of her cases. He had always been fair and often sympathetic. He had been particularly sensitive in dealing with the murder of Randall Tye. One of the few reporters who did not accept the obvious indications of a drug overdose as the cause of Randall's death, Timothy

Nass had withheld judgment. He'd been sympathetic with Norah's effort to vindicate the man she'd loved.

She had both Timothy Nass's home and office numbers. She decided to try home first.

The line rang four times then the message machine cut in. Resigned, Norah began, "This is Lieutenant Mulcahaney, Homicide Fourth Zone, Mr. Nass. I have something very important to discuss with you. Please call me when you get in no matter what time . . ."

"Timothy Nass, Lieutenant," he cut in overriding the machine. "What can I do for you?"

"Sorry to disturb you, Mr. Nass. I need your help."

BRAVE BOY SOUGHT TO I.D. GRANDMA'S KILLER

The story appeared in the morning edition. The headline, along with Todd Millard's picture, filled the tabloid's entire front page. Inside on page three, another headline:

CHILD SOLE WITNESS TO FATAL ATTACK

Police Appeal to Boy to Step Forward

"We have made an arrest," Lieutenant Norah Mulcahaney, in charge of the investigation into the murder of the legendary star, Wilma Danay, told this reporter. "We believe we have the killer, but the evidence is not conclusive. Todd was there. He saw the killer. He stood face-to-face with the murderer and can make a positive identification. That would guarantee a conviction."

Todd Millard is missing and has been since the night of his grandmother's murder. Lieutenant Mulcahaney believes the boy ran away because he was afraid and that he's been hiding since out of fear. She wants Todd to know that there's no reason to be afraid anymore.

The killer is locked up. "He can't hurt you," Lieutenant Mulcahaney promises.

She wants Todd to know that he can call her office at any time and she'll go and get him wherever he is. "I'll be waiting right here by this telephone. Please, contact me, Todd. We need your evidence."

Norah's picture accompanied the part of the story on page three.

The other papers picked up the appeal and published it in the later editions. Radio carried it through the day and TV reported it at night.

Norah remained in her office trying to conduct normal business, but every time there was a knock at the door, her heart jumped. Every time the phone rang, her throat went dry. Communications had orders to cut into any conversation at any time if the boy was on the line; nevertheless she was nervous and impatient when her line was in use.

She was as gentle as she could be with the parents. "You've made your appeal on television," she reminded the Millards. "It didn't work. Give this a chance. Don't make any more statements. Don't say anything. Please."

At the precinct the word was out to keep off Norah's line, so the phone on her desk rang less and less frequently as the day dragged on. There were fewer and fewer knocks at her door. She should have gone off duty at four, but she didn't. Nobody expected she would. At eight, without being asked, Ferdi brought in a tuna on whole wheat and coffee, no sugar, and placed the bag in front of Norah.

"I'll be at my desk," he told her.

His shift was over, too, but she didn't send him home.

A little after midnight, Timothy Nass called. His normally gruff voice sounded gentle.

"Anything?"

"No."

"Ten-year-old boys don't read newspapers and they don't watch TV newscasts."

"I know. I was hoping an adult would see the story and recognize his picture."

"Sure. Listen, I'd like to do a follow-up, but I need a new development, something to hang it on."

"I don't have anything."

"I'm sorry."

"You did your best. I'm grateful."

"If anything comes up . . ."

"I'll be in touch," she promised.

Somehow, they managed to squeeze a cot into her office and Norah lay down for a few hours. She didn't sleep.

The next day dragged even more slowly than the first. Jim Felix called to renew his support. Captain Jacoby looked in at least three times. Food appeared in front of her. She ate it without noticing it. She conducted the routine business of the squad.

Night came. The squad room quieted. Norah put her head down on the desk. She didn't hear the light knock at her door. She didn't know anyone had come in till the desk sergeant touched her shoulder and shook it gently.

"Lieutenant . . ."

Two shapeless figures stood in the shadows beyond the light of her desk lamp like figures out of the mists of her dreams. The woman was small, rotund, layered in tatters from the scarf over her head to the strips of cloth wound like puttees around her legs. She was leading a boy by the hand; small, thin, in clothes that were too large—trousers dragging at the heels, jacket reaching to his knees; shabby, but clean. His hair had once been blond but was now brown. A bad dye job, Norah thought. His sneakers were cut out at the toes.

"Lieutenant, these people asked for you."

"Thanks, Sergeant," she replied without looking at him. She had eyes only for the child.

"Todd? Todd Millard?"

The boy didn't reply. He looked to his companion.

"Yes, ma'am. That's who he is." The woman nudged him forward.

"There's nothing to be afraid of," Norah assured him.

"He knows that." The woman gave him another gentle push forward. He resisted, holding on to her hand.

"How long has he been with you?" Norah asked.

"A couple of weeks, a month . . . I don't know. Time don't mean much anymore. I noticed him riding the train one night. It was close to midnight. I know that because that's when they start rousting us. Anyhow, he was in his pajamas and alone. I could tell he'd never been on the trains before— he didn't know enough to get off before the end of the line. If you ride to the last stop, the cops put you out on the street and it's real hard to get back down again. So we rode together till morning. Then I said so long and went up by myself like always. That night when I got back, he was waiting for me. He was waiting right in the same spot where I'd left him."

"Did you know who he was? What he was doing all alone?"

"He didn't tell me and I didn't ask."

"Flyers with his picture have been all over the neighborhood, all over the city."

The woman shrugged.

"You didn't see his parents on television last week asking about him?"

She shook her head. "I got no place to watch television."

"His mother offered a twenty-five-thousand-dollar reward for information about him."

"I didn't bring him in to sell him."

"Then why did you bring him in?"

"You said you needed him as a witness to his grandma's murder, isn't that right?"

"Yes." Norah nodded. "Please, sit down." She placed chairs for them. Then from the top right-hand drawer of the desk, she removed a file, selected a half-dozen four-by-six glossies and laid them out in front of Todd. "Was the person who hurt your grandmother one of these?"

The boy peered intently and after a very short consideration pointed confidently. "Him."

He'd selected the photograph of Henry Lancelot, which they'd obtained from his agent.

"Are you sure?"

"Yes, ma'am."

"But it was dark, wasn't it? The lights in your room were out, weren't they? And so were the lights in the hall."

"Yes, ma'am. He put them back on."

"Ah. . . ." She was testing his memory as well as his ability to withstand unfriendly interrogation on the witness stand. "But he was disguised. He was wearing a stocking mask."

The boy was not at all shaken. "He pulled it off. He said he couldn't see through it."

"What did he do with it?"

"Stuffed it in his pocket."

She was satisfied.

"Is that all?" Todd Millard asked.

"For now. You'll have to identify the man in court. Will you be able to do that?"

"Yes."

"You won't be afraid?"

"No, ma'am."

That wasn't true, Norah thought. He would be afraid, but he would go through with it. "Good."

Todd stood up and the woman stood up with him. "May we go now, please?"

Norah was taken aback. She hadn't expected this. She had assumed . . . she realized she hadn't thought past the boy's coming in. She didn't know how to respond. She looked to the woman who had cared for Todd and who had brought him in. She was silent. Squat and shapeless in her rags, she was cloaked in dignity.

"Your mother and father are waiting for you," Norah told the boy. "Don't you want to go home?"

"You mean we're going to live together, the three of us like a family?"

And now Norah also understood Richard Millard's television appeal to his son. But what could she say? The divorce had made the child bitter. In his time of danger and of need neither parent had been there for him. She couldn't lie.

"If you mean will the three of you live together in the same house, I can't say. I don't know."

"Then it'll be like it was before. They'll fight and yell at each other. They'll argue about who I should stay with, but neither one really wants me. In the end, with Nana gone, it'll turn out to be boarding school for me."

"I don't think so. They do love you, Todd, and I believe they've learned they have to share you. And you have to accept that."

His lips trembled. "Ruth wants me. Ruth and I . . . we have fun together."

Of course! Norah thought. Of course. She kept forgetting he was only a ten-year-old child, not an adult. His standards were not those of an adult. His Nana had spent time with him; they'd had fun together. To him it was the indication that she cared. And now this lonely, homeless woman had taken him to her heart. She'd taught him how to survive underground; she'd made a game of it. They'd had fun and to him that was proof of her love.

"They're your parents, Todd, and maybe they don't show

it, but they do love you. Give them another chance." She held out her hand. "Let me take you to them."

Todd looked at Norah for a long time, then he turned to the woman who had protected him and cared for him and shared her subsistence with him. "Ruth?"

"They're your folks. You should give them a second chance," she replied without hesitation.

He hugged her. Then on tiptoe, he reached up and kissed her wrinkled mouth. Having done so, he turned his back resolutely and took Norah's hand.

She spoke through the intercom to Ferdi Arenas. "Tell the Millards we're on our way."

Holding his small moist hand in hers, Norah led the boy through the squad room and out to the elevator. Somewhere deep inside her a small, hard lump encapsulating pain and regret had grown over the years. In this moment she could feel it start to melt and the yearning spread through her whole being. She wished she could take Todd home with her. Keep him. Raise him, teach him, care for him, love him, make sure he was never frightened again. Make sure he would always be safe.

The child stepped close, not nestling against her, but definitely craving protection and comfort. She wanted to draw him to her, hug him, hold him. Her heart nearly broke with the need, but she only gave his hand an extra squeeze.

Norah's instructions to the Millards had been to wait at home, promising they would be notified if—when—Todd came in. Adele Millard's apartment was nearest to the station, only a short drive, so that was where Norah now took him. She spotted the Millards from a block away. At Ferdi's message they had come down and were waiting on the street, standing close together, looking in every direction. As she pulled up on the other side, Todd saw them, too. He opened his door and ran out into the traffic.

"No, Todd, wait!" Norah cried and ran after him.

Paying no attention to her or to the blaring horns or screeching brakes, he ran straight into his mother's open arms. After several moments, she passed him on to his father. The three held on to each other. They had forgotten Norah.

She stopped, biting back the tears. This child was lucky, she thought; he had people who despite their differences cared for him and had learned they must put his welfare first. There were others not so fortunate—abandoned children, rejected, abused. So many other children. Slowly, Norah turned back to her car. Surely somewhere there would be a child for her.